"Let's make lo[ve]

Brian pulled Ashb[y] [...]
sight of her slim body wrapped [...]
pink, skintight bodysuit running ahead of
him had turned his thoughts to a much more
intimate form of exercise.

Ashby glanced around. "Here? We're five
miles from home."

His lips nuzzled her mouth, coaxing,
teasing. She tasted as fresh as the springlike
day. The ache in him grew and he rasped,
"This is driving me crazy. If we don't get
home soon I'll . . ."

"You'll what?" she teased.

"Drag you over there into the bushes."

She stepped away from him, her heart
beating as if she had already crossed the
finish line. "We'll race. Give me a thirty-
second lead?"

He nodded impatiently.

"What's the winner get?"

A wicked smile crossed his face. "The
winner gets to act out his or her favorite
erotic fantasy. . . ."

Marilynne Rudick dreamed about competing in a marathon but decided it would be more practical to invent characters who were marathon runners and have them do the work. But after reading countless books on the sport, attending races and writing draft after draft of *Glory Days*, she's now convinced training for and running the marathon would have been much easier. Marilynne was especially intrigued by the element of competition within a marriage—and her resolution in the story is the ultimate romantic fantasy for the 1990s.

Marilynne and her attorney husband make their home in Maryland.

Books by Marilynne Rudick
HARLEQUIN TEMPTATION
127–SEEING IS BELIEVING

Glory Days

MARILYNNE RUDICK

Harlequin Books

TORONTO • NEW YORK • LONDON
AMSTERDAM • PARIS • SYDNEY • HAMBURG
STOCKHOLM • ATHENS • TOKYO • MILAN

To Amanda, Jean, Lorrie and Earl,
friends who went the distance

Published July 1990

ISBN 0-373-25408-3

1

THEY CALLED IT the wall; Ashby O'Hara called it living hell. In all her years of running, in her nine previous marathons, she had somehow miraculously escaped this dreaded curse that turned bodies to aching, throbbing protoplasm and worse, turned minds to defeat. Now she had hit the wall, and it was more horrible than she'd imagined.

At twenty miles she had run tentatively and tensely for a few minutes, as she always did at that juncture, half expecting to crash against the invisible barrier that transformed certain victory into anguishing defeat. The collision had not come, and giving a long sigh of relief, she'd run nearly effortlessly, her mind clear, focusing on her single goal: winning. In private celebration, Ashby had increased her pace. She was immune. Euphoria anesthetized her to the normal pain of the 26.2-mile trek. She ran like a doe, surely and gracefully, the thick ribbon of spectators dissolving into a colorful blur around her.

She steeled herself for the home stretch, the final lonely miles after Hains Point, when spectators were scarce and fierce winds battered her face. But she was impervious to setbacks. Checking her watch at the twenty-two-mile point, she'd given silent thanks to the gods of running. Ashby could scarcely believe it—she was ahead of her pace.

"Looking good," a lone spectator had called. "You're number three."

Not good enough, she thought. That meant Sheila Grayson, who had started out in front, and Marit Lingstrom, Sweden's Olympic hopeful, who had passed her four miles back, were still in the race. It had been too much to hope they'd drop out. Victory would not be that easy. How far ahead? she wondered. She'd find out soon enough. If she intended to win, Ashby had but one choice—to pick up her pace once again, to run all out, as if her life depended on it. Indeed it did.

Then it happened—without warning, without reason—as if a time bomb had detonated, racking her body, sending her legs sprawling in opposite directions, her arms flailing wildly above her head. Daggers pierced her calves. Sharp cramps had her doubled over. Nausea swept through her. The world disappeared. She no longer heard the thud of feet around her. Washington's Tidal Basin became a blurred puddle. *I'm going to faint. Please, just a few more miles.*

Her lips, suddenly parched, uttered a faint curse. *Why today, when it's so important?* She took a deep breath and willed her body to run, then just to move, to stand upright. Her breathing collapsed. She had no choice; she could not go on. Not an ounce of strength remained. She wanted to stretch out on the cool grass, to feel its caressing strokes, its seductive softness. To rest, to sleep. She jerked her head upward. It would be the end of her dream. *Their* dream.

"Ashby... Ashby."

The voice grew more insistent until, penetrating her consciousness, it became recognizable.

Slowly she focused her eyes on a crown of curly, brown hair and intense blue eyes...a lanky frame, leaning on a well-worn ten-speed. Dan Lyons, a friend, a fellow athlete, a welcome sight. She tried for a smile, but failed miserably.

"Oh, Dan. I can't. Please...help."

He took her hand and carefully wrapped it around a plastic cup, coaxing a straw between her lips.

"Drink it slowly and keep moving."

"Dan, it's all over."

"Ashby." Dan's voice range with urgency. "Listen to me. He's won. Brian came in first."

"First!" Dan's words sent a surge of electricity through Ashby. She sprang upright, color leaped to her cheeks, then drained away, leaving them pure white; clenching her side, she bent like a felled willow.

Dan poured the contents of his water bottle over her head. "This'll help." The cool water shivered down her shoulders, and like the first slap on a baby's bottom, brought her back to life.

"He's won," she mumbled. "Just like he promised. And I'm..."

"More good news, Champ," Dan continued. "Sheila's out. Pulled muscle. Just the Swedish streak left."

"How far ahead?" The question was instinctive, coming from somewhere inside, beyond fatigue, deeper than pain.

"Within catching distance." A wide grin creased Dan's face. "You can get her on the hill. It's up to you now, Champ."

The Hill. Ashby's tour de force. The last mile of the race was a steady uphill to the Iwo Jima statue. A cruel end. But Ashby had trained on Boston's Heartbreak

Hill, the marathon runner's Waterloo. How many times had Brian made her run up that roller coaster of hills? She'd cursed him all the way. Until suddenly she'd learned its secret—slowing down before the upgrade, gathering energy for a powerful burst. It had become her forte, her secret weapon.

"Oh God, but how am I gonna get to the hill?" she moaned.

"One foot in front of the other," Dan advised calmly. He patted her affectionately on the shoulder. "You'll make it, Champ. One more thing—Brian said to tell you he loves you."

BRIAN O'HARA slipped away from the press, needing a few minutes to himself. The euphoria of his own win had passed, and his excitement had turned to worry. It was damn hot, a brilliant, Indian summer day, the kind that made Washington's cherry trees flirt with the idea of blooming again, and sapped the strength of runners. Heat was Ashby's nemesis. A snowbird, she plowed through knee-deep snowdrifts. But could she handle seventy-two degrees in mid-November...Brian lifted his shoulders in a helpless gesture. "Unnatural," he thought.

Brian had heard that Ashby had hit the wall. Dan's troubled face confirmed it, although he'd assured Brian that Ashby was just fine. "She'll finish," he'd predicted. Brian didn't dare ask if he thought she might be the first woman finisher.

Suddenly it all seemed crazy. Was the sacrifice worth the reward? Just the thought of Ashby bent over in pain was enough to make him call the whole thing off. Kids' stuff. A fool's dream. Why was he driven? Worse, why had he pulled Ashby into this?

Not winning might prove to be a blessing. If Ashby came in first, this would only be the beginning of a grueling odyssey. Five torturous months to train for the Boston Marathon; if their times qualified, another uphill battle to the Olympic trials a year later. And if all went well, perhaps, just maybe, a few days of glory. Could the pain and sacrifice possibly be worth it? Would it be better to give it up now, return to Boston and a normal life, and run for nothing more than pure fun?

He could always go on by himself. It would be much easier if he was the only one involved. No crazy schedules to juggle. No need to worry if it was all too much for Ashby. No guilt about what running was doing to *her* life. No worry about her injuries, her future. He sighed. No fun at all.

He didn't want to go it alone. Running by himself had been nothing more than endurance, an egotistical struggle for physical perfection, an empty obsession. Life had been centered around his training routine, his mileage, his pulled muscles, his diet and his trophies. Ashby had turned all that around. She had given him the gift of sharing. He felt joy when he ran with Ashby, a sense of oneness. It had enabled him to know her as well as he knew himself. When they ran together, he was as conscious of her heartbeat as he was of his own; he felt her pulse beating life into his body. He knew every muscle, every fiber of her body intimately. And along with knowing her body came knowing her mind. The connection was almost mystical. And that was why in spite of his win—a victory that should have made him giddy with joy—he was in such pain.

THE PAIN did not lessen. Ashby's feet hit the pavement like jackhammers sending brutal spasms through her body. But somehow Dan's advice was consolingly simple. *Don't worry about the finish, just put one foot in front of the other.*

And there were Dan's other words. "Brian says to tell you he loves you." How could she fail Brian? He had never failed her. He was always there—straightforward, honest and boldly courageous. Brian, who never uttered the word "impossible." Brian, who didn't know the meaning of failure. How had she ever lived without him? He was the one who had seen the potential in her running. More than that, he had convinced her that she could be more than good—that she could be great.

Miraculously she was gaining strength. The nausea was gone. Her head was clearing; once again she could focus on monitoring her body, on reading the race. Two miles until the final climb. She'd have to hope that Marit was not too far ahead, to gamble that her final, uphill drive would not come too late. How much time had she lost in her semiconscious state? Had any other women passed her? Ashby dared not look behind to see who was on her tail. It would be a psychological disaster.

She was feeling better now, and her impulse was to run fast to make up for lost time. But she knew her well-being was precarious, her sense of strength elusive. "Stay strong, relax," she repeated, as if chanting a mantra.

Her near collapse had cost her precious minutes, leaving no hope now of bettering her own marathon time. The heat; she hadn't trained for the heat. She could only hope that Marit, also from a northern clime, was finding the unseasonable temperature difficult. Remembering a trick Brian had taught her, Ashby imagined herself running through the snow toward the finish line, bundled in a down coat. It helped; the heat seemed to lift.

A crowd had gathered at the Pentagon as she made her final approach into Arlington. "Doing fine...you're gaining." She sensed the electricity in their voices; it gave her strength. They were with her, caught up in her fantasy—hers and Brian's. The crowd was anxious to share their win.

Suddenly her knees buckled as she glimpsed a golden mane, flying in the wind. She caught her breath and stared, mesmerized by the even pace of the long, graceful legs. If Marit Lingstrom had come anywhere near the wall, if she felt any pain or had fought any battles with the heat, there was no evidence of it. No wonder they called her the Swedish streak! She looked as fresh as dawn. Would Marit ever slow down? How could she even catch, much less pass her?

Now Ashby had no time to gather strength, to pace herself and hope to overtake Marit on the hill. Marit Lingstrom would finish before Ashby O'Hara made her great surge. Her throat dried to parchment, her legs trembled, not from exhaustion, but from sheer nerves. She took a deep breath; adrenaline spurted into her veins. She moved in what felt like double time. It was now or never.

BRIAN STOOD at the top of the hill and helplessly scanned the horde of runners streaming toward the finish line. Anxiety was written in every tight muscle of his strong, Irish face. At a time like this he would have preferred anonymity. Success was a mixed blessing; he was surrounded by the press. Like vultures, they had descended upon him as soon as they heard Ashby was gaining. Brian was angry; there was equal drama in her win or defeat. They were just here for the fight, to write about the blood.

Although he had changed from his sweat-soaked running clothes, Brian could not stop shivering. He dreaded the moment when the first woman would come into view, fearing that he would not see Ashby's dark hair, her small, pliant body. How many times had he stood on the top of a hill, craning to catch sight of Ashby as she fought her way uphill? The first glimpse always filled him with fierce pride. Now he would give anything to see her.

Anything for just a glimpse of her damp hair, plastered against high cheekbones. Anything to catch sight of her sapphire eyes, inky with determination. Right now nothing would be as welcome as seeing Ashby's good-luck singlet, its once bold Boston Brahmin now faded to a quiet beige. Soaking with sweat, the singlet would cling to her small breasts that rose and fell with each deep breath. Under her shirt was something special that the crowds and the press would never see, and the very thought of it lifted Brian's spirits. On a long chain that hung close to her heart was a small, gold #1. Brian had given it to her after her first marathon. She hadn't won. She hadn't even come close. But in his life Ashby O'Hara was number one.

The crowd stirred. Bored photographers bounded to life. A lump rose in his throat and his heart seemed to stop. He heard Dan's voice before he was capable of making any sound.

"Oh, God."

Brian could barely look. "How is she?" he rasped.

"Hanging in." A pause hung thickly in the air. "They're neck and neck."

BONE WEARY, Ashby had finally caught the Swedish streak. How, she never knew. Long ago she had exhausted her supply of glycogen. Her second wind had come and gone. All that was left was pure grit, sheer determination. But by some miracle she was still running. With her body totally depleted, her mind took charge. Suddenly she felt as if she was running with someone else's body.

The last mile. All uphill. She only hoped that this stranger's body would last through the final stretch. But regardless of whose body, she was running with Brian's soul. For a precious second her concentration strayed from her preoccupation with Marit, and she strained to catch a glimpse of Brian. Like an addict, she needed a quick fix—a reassuring glimpse of his tall, lean frame, thick, chestnut hair straying down his forehead, brows knit together above stormy, green eyes, etched lines that would soften with relief when he saw her. That would get her up the hill. It always did. But would it get her up first?

BRIAN'S HEART ACHED. So close. So close. He couldn't bear to watch her. Exhaustion was written in every step, every stumble. He knew how it felt to be plumb empty, running on sheer nerve. Oh, he hoped she knew he was with her, every mile, every step. Ashby couldn't possibly win. Marit was as fresh as a daisy; soon she would break away, make her final push. Damn, how he wanted the win. He tried to tell himself that it didn't matter, he didn't care. Other things in life were more important. He slammed his fist hard into his palm. Whom was he fooling? He wanted it. Wanted it badly. He could taste victory—their victory. He wanted a try at the Olympics, and he wanted to do it with Ashby. It was their goal, their triumph. Theirs together. His eyes clouded with tears and he did not bother to wipe them away. He could not bear to think of the end.

"She's pulling ahead."

Brian hunched his shoulders forward. He could not bring himself to watch.

He felt a sharp elbow, then Dan's voice. "It's the Champ. She's in the lead."

Brian crashed through the line of Marine guards, straining for a closer look.

"Come on, Ashby. Oh, Babe, just a few more steps."

He knew she couldn't hear his plea above the crowd's deafening roar. But for an instant, she looked up, raising her head, proud and erect. Somehow she picked him out of the crowd. Their eyes met, and he saw a flicker of hope. She lengthened her stride. Sweat poured down her brow, clouding narrowed eyes; she clenched her jaw in fierce determination.

"Two lengths ahead!"

The Swedish streak coolly closed the distance. Teeth gritted, Ashby slowly inched out in front.

"Oh, Babe, just a few more inches."

THE PHOTOGRAPHER captured the instant that Ashby's chest broke through the tape, head erect, hair blowing wildly in the wind, arms high in the air, her legs spread in a final, proud leap. Those legs were covered with mud, her shirt was stained with sweat. Her face, red with exhaustion, was creased with pain. Brian would treasure this picture always.

He threw his arms around her; his own tears of pure joy mingled with her salty sweat. He had never seen Ashby O'Hara look more beautiful.

2

FOR A QUIET MOMENT Brian stood motionless over the sleeping figure, her stomach pressed against the mattress, the thick, quilted comforter molding the soft curve of her derriere. Her hair, starkly black against the white sheets, fanned across her face. Both arms were stretched over her head in a wide V. Victory, he mused. Even in sleep. He paused before waking her, following the slight, even movements of her breathing. Peaceful, so peaceful. Ashby seemed dwarfed by the king-size bed. Alone, so lonely and vulnerable. Brian had an urge to crawl back into bed and wrap her in his arms. To keep her warm and safe.

He placed a glass of orange juice, freshly squeezed, and two extra-strength aspirins on the nightstand. His hand reached for the nape of her neck, one of the places he loved to touch. Hidden by her shoulder-length hair, it was smooth, like the skin of a newborn.

How different she looked today. Yesterday she'd been Ashby O'Hara, a human dynamo—one hundred pounds of pure energy, blazing her way uphill. Then he'd noticed only her strong legs, threaded with firm muscles; the long arms, moving like pendulums at her side, a frame lean and sparse—a perfect runner's body. Had that woman anything in common with this one— Suzanne Ashby Clayton O'Hara? Fragile, like her mother's tea set—the heirloom cups with the fine gold leaf and the tiny red flowers.

"Time to get up." He bent his head to her ear and couldn't resist running his tongue along the shell-like curve.

"Hmm." Ashby gave an inadvertent sigh of pleasure and smiled. She yawned, stretching her hands lazily above her. "Brian, what time is it?"

"Almost ten."

Ashby shifted tentatively, giving way to a low groan. Cautiously she opened first one eye, then the other. She lifted her head slightly off the pillow, then collapsed into its downy softness. "Ohhh . . ."

"What hurts?" His very voice massaged her, much like the fingers that were running along the stiff blades of her shoulders.

Ashby curled into a tight ball, then sat up, her movements studied and cautious. "I think it would be easier if I just told you what didn't hurt."

"What's the worst?"

"No contest. My head." Her brows came together as she tentatively rubbed the offending temples. "I feel like I ran the race upside down."

Brian's laugh was deep. "That," he said, "is not from running." He placed the juice and aspirins firmly in her hand.

"I was afraid of that. Champagne. A lot?"

"Let's just say, Champ, that you went the distance."

"It seemed to help at the time." She raised her eyes as she quietly recalled the previous evening. "So many toasts."

"And so many bars," he added dryly.

"It was wonderful!" Her lips curved as memory returned. "Brian, we did it!"

"Sure did!"

"By the skin of our teeth." An uncomfortable picture of Marit crossing the finish line, literally on her heels, flashed through Ashby's mind. She shivered.

"We never thought it would be easy."

"I never thought it would be this hard. Or painful. How are you?" She looked up, catching his terrific grin.

"Never been better."

"No soreness, no aches?"

"Sure, the usual things. But they feel wonderful. Reminders of victory."

Ashby pulled one leg from beneath the covers and began kneading the taut muscles of her calf. "I think I could do with a few less reminders."

"You'll feel great by tomorrow."

"Is that another of Brian O'Hara's famous promises?"

"It comes with a guarantee."

"Save me from the charming Irish." She looked up again, her eyes fondly caressing Brian's Celtic features—square chin, strong cheekbones and green eyes sometimes as soft as moss, other times as cool as jade. "How long have you been up?"

"Hours," he admitted. "Couldn't sleep. I've been thinking about our next race."

Ashby fell against the pillows. "Count me out, O'Hara. I'll never race again."

"That's what you said last time." He bent down and bestowed a gentle pat on her bare rump. "Out of the sack, sleepyhead."

"Slave driver! Can't we take today off?"

"Sorry," he said apologetically, "there's the interview with *American Sports*. Very important."

"That's right. I can hardly believe it. Last week I couldn't get my magazine subscription renewed. Today, the famed Ted McDowell. What time?"

"Noon."

"I'll never make it!"

"You've got plenty of time—almost enough to run another marathon."

"Please, don't even mention that word."

"A hot bath will fix you right up," Brian promised. "It's the kind you like—those whirlpool jobs with bubbles and sprays."

"Paradise!" Ashby swung her legs around and gingerly planted them on the ground. "Hey, Brian, will you call room service and order some strong coffee?"

"Certainly. Nothing is too good for the woman who beat the Swedish streak."

ASHBY SLIPPED into the oversize Jacuzzi, reveling in the hot, sudsy water. She stretched luxuriantly. She always loved the day after a race. Normally it was a timeless day—no schedule, no training. A whole day of sweet indulgence.

On the day after a race anything seemed possible: the Boston Marathon, qualifying for the Olympics, an Olympic medal. She could do it. She and Brian.

She reached for the morning newspaper, which lay on the tile floor. Turning to the sports section, she devoured every word about the race. She'd gotten most of the attention. "Stunning upset," the paper had called it. Yet what she'd done wasn't all that remarkable. Her time wasn't record breaking. With the exception of Marit, the competition had been second-rate.

She tossed the paper back onto the floor. The press had missed the real story. Brian was responsible for both wins, his and hers. In every race Ashby inevitably faced a black moment, when her desire to quit was greater than her desire to win. And always it was Brian who made the difference, who transformed that moment of defeat into victory. Without Brian she would not have won.

For weeks Ashby had dreamed over and over again of winning. She'd imagined celebrating at party after party. Now that was all behind her; in the silence of the morning after she'd discovered a simple truth. Public celebrations and acknowledgments were unimportant. Victory was personal and private, and she longed for an intimate celebration with the only person who mattered.

The door opened. Brian, carrying a huge tray, stood on the threshold. He wore his familiar faded jeans and his favorite sweater, a pale blue crewneck with the elbows nearly rubbed out. She always nagged at him to replace it, but in truth she kind of liked the look. It was soft and comfortable, and seemed molded to his long, lean body.

"Coffee, tea or me?" he drawled.

She lifted a brow slightly. "With the right stimulant I could skip the coffee."

"And what did you have in mind, Mrs. O'Hara?"

"Tea?"

"We're all out."

He turned, placing the tray on a chair. As he bent at the waist, his bottom pressed against his jeans, curv-

ing in a sensual half circle. World-class buns, she
thought fondly, and smothered an urge to reach out and
run her hands against the soft denim. Instead she
watched in delicious anticipation as he pulled the
sweater over his head, revealing first a taut waist that
broadened to a muscular V. A thick mat of hair covered his chest. He reached for the zipper on his pants
and struggled to work it down, then pulled two long,
sinewy legs free and wrestled out of white cotton briefs.

Ashby felt her breathing quicken as her eyes did a
languorous sweep. As always she was awed by his
body, which was as perfect as a classic sculpture. But
posed statues never captured his vibrancy, his passion.
Athlete, lover, husband. She knew all three men intimately: an athlete obsessed with excellence, a lover
who burned with passion, a husband secure enough to
shelter and nourish.

"How's the water?" He ran his fingers through the
suds.

"Surf's up." Ashby laughed, deliberately splashing a
handful of water at him. It landed on his chest and ran
down in a thin line to his navel.

He retaliated, scooping up water and throwing it over
her head.

It caused a shiver. "Truce," she said and giggled. "I
give up."

"Hmm. If only the competition knew the secret."

"Don't you dare tell how easily I surrender to tall
runners with a certain Irish charm."

"For a price I'll keep it a secret."

"Name your price."

He flicked a brow upward as he regarded her submerged body. "Let's just say we're talking about a floating currency."

Brian's mouth curled with pleasure as his mind filled in the tantalizing details of the body obscured by the soapy water: a graceful neck, narrow shoulders and high breasts that fitted snugly into his palms; a long torso, a belly button hidden in a flat stomach, slender thighs and calves threaded with muscles. He marveled at the contrasts of her body, soft and tender, hard and sturdy. And his thoughts filled him with desire.

It was more than physical desire. His heart swelled with admiration. Even the word "love" did not begin to touch his feelings. Yesterday he had struggled to tell her how he felt, but words had failed him. Still, there were ways that went beyond words.

"Is there room for two?" he asked huskily.

"The last time I said yes to anything," Ashby told him with a laugh, "you had me running twenty-six miles."

"Don't worry," he promised, his eyes glinting. "This time I don't think you'll have any trouble going the distance."

He hesitated before lowering himself into the tub. For an instant Brian felt as shy and awkward as an adolescent. He knew every inch of her intimately, from the birthmark on her left thigh to the dimple in her bottom. Suddenly it was all new, all different. Yesterday had changed everything. From somewhere unknown to Brian she'd found a cache of supernatural stamina, strength and courage. How much more was there still to learn? he wondered. And the thought both awed and excited him. And somehow it frightened him just a bit.

Sudsy water reached the rim of the rub as Brian settled into the Jacuzzi. Facing each other they moved gingerly, the water lapping over the sides at each cautious slither. "Where's it hurt?" he asked.

She laughed, lifting a muscled leg and wiggling her toes. "Even my big toe hurts."

"I've just the remedy." His fingers worked their way up the stiff calf, as they'd done hundreds of times before. The familiar ritual comforted, and he breathed easier.

Ashby uttered a long, low sigh. "Magic fingers," she whispered.

"Please insert another quarter."

"I want the whole dollar's worth."

His pressure softened to soothing, then playful strokes. Plantar fascia, Achilles, gastrocnemius, hamstring. Clinical terms that somehow never seemed to describe Ashby's high-arched, narrow foot, her smoothly curved calf, nor her ankle, secretly ticklish. He felt her tense muscles relax. Her moans changed to a soft purr. As his fingers wandered up her thigh, Latin nomenclature drifted from his mind.

Ashby leaned forward, running her hands in long strokes against his rock-hard muscles. Her fingers moved from the sensitive soles of his feet along the bundled fingers of his calf to the crook of his knee.

"Torture, pure torture," he said with a sigh, curving his lips.

She lifted her hands for an instant and arched a brow. "Shall I stop?"

"Don't you dare," he rasped.

Her hands massaged his inner thigh. She played against the strained fibers much as a gypsy musician worked the strings of a tired violin, eliciting first whines and creaks, then finally a joyous harmony.

Brian pulled her close; wet tendrils splashed against his chest, sending a delicious shiver down his spine. He pulled her still nearer, caressing the tender muscles of her neck, then her shoulders, the slippery water lubricating each stroke. Her body arched, a small, contented sigh escaped her lips.

He met her waiting mouth with a first, tender kiss. Like the pattern of his hands, his kiss was soothing at first. Then the rhythm changed. No longer was the caress therapeutic, the mood healing. Passion deepened, kept urgent time with the beating of their hearts; legs wound around hips; water splashed high into the air. Ashby's breasts pressed against his chest, the airy bubbles soothing its wiry roughness.

Brian ached with tenderness; he felt as though his heart would burst. He struggled to find words, the right words, any words, but only a deep sigh emerged.

Ashby's lips moved against his, quelling his private anguish. "I know, I understand," she whispered.

Brian pulled Ashby atop his long body and cradled her curves against him. They twisted and turned; water tumbled over the sides of the tub, thoroughly soaking the clothes lazily thrown aside. They never noticed.

The aches of yesterday were gone. Passion, like a powerful drug, numbed the trauma left behind by twenty-six hard miles. In a fiery moment the previous night's celebration became what it had been meant to be: a hollow prelude. Herculean triumphs and Olympic hopes faded as they reveled in a private conquest no less awesome than their public triumph.

At long last they rejoiced in their own, intimate celebration.

ASHBY THOUGHT that Ted McDowell, contentedly sipping scotch under the palms and fronds of the hotel restaurant looked strangely out of place—too tough and weathered for such a tony setting. However, he seemed unperturbed by the O'Haras' late arrival, and when Ashby caught sight of a sleek young blonde, who seemed to melt away as they appeared, she thought she knew why.

Ashby herself felt anything but sleek in black trousers and a turquoise sweater, with a wide, batik scarf wrapped turban-style around her hair. She hadn't meant the effect to be exotic; her hair just hadn't had time to dry. She flushed as she and Brian exchanged wide grins.

McDowell was a legendary figure. He'd been around for what seemed like always and was famous for his incisive, often acerbic profiles. Both his awesome reputation and the knowledge that this interview was crucial made Ashby feel ill at ease.

Although McDowell had requested a quiet table, the O'Haras could not escape notice as they made their way toward him. Ashby tried to appear nonchalant, but couldn't suppress a broad smile, and she found it difficult to glide gracefully across the room on legs that refused to bend.

"Great race!" exclaimed McDowell when they'd ordered drinks and a light lunch. Pointing to her head, Ashby declined anything more alcoholic than club soda. Nodding sympathetically, McDowell pulled a tape recorder from a satchel and set it on the table. In spite of the man's cordiality, Ashby felt her stomach tighten when she heard the dim whir of the machine.

"Let's start with background," suggested McDowell. "Tell me, how'd you two meet?"

"The hospital, almost five years ago," Ashby explained, relieved by the friendly beginning. "I'd been appointed to a committee to raise money for a new children's clinic, and all of a sudden this new, hotshot administrator showed up. First time I'd ever seen him."

Brian suppressed a smile. He'd noticed her weeks before at the hospital's Christmas party, his attention caught by her high-spirited laugh.

Brian had never suffered from an underdose of confidence and he'd never had problems attracting women. They seemed to like his tall, athletic frame and his somewhat rough features. Even his nose—broken three times in ice hockey matches—seemed to engender female admiration. But he had found Miss Clayton very intimidating. Somehow he felt big and clumsy around her. There was something else—uppity Bostonian—he'd thought. Later he had softened; she was just majestic.

He soon found out she was a physical therapist. Odd work for such a delicate woman he had thought. And she was elusive. She seemed to disappear. Every time he ventured into the physical therapy department on some flimsy pretext or other, she'd be off to some far corner of Boston—outpatient therapy, he was told. He'd just about abandoned hope when she showed up at the fund-raising meeting.

"Love at first sight, or did he run after you? Figuratively speaking," McDowell probed.

"Neither," Ashby corrected him. "I didn't even know he was interested. Then one day I suggested the hospital sponsor a fun run as a way to raise money. To my amazement, Brian not only thought it was terrific, but he suggested we cochair it."

Brian grinned. "I'd spent weeks trying to figure out how to get to know the elusive Miss Clayton, and all of a sudden she suggested doing the thing I loved most. I almost fell off my chair."

"And you agreed to be cochairmen?"

"Reluctantly," Ashby confided. "I sized him up as a typical jock. I suspected *he*'d get the glory and *I*'d do the work."

"Ashby drew up a plan with assigned tasks before she agreed. Tough cookie," Brian said, grinning.

"We started working together on the race, having drinks after meetings, an occasional pizza, then one day Brian produced two tickets to a Bruins game."

"Were you a fan?"

"Not really."

"But you went, anyway?"

She grinned. "By that time I was ready to go anywhere he asked."

To her astonishment, she'd loved the game. By the second period she was standing with her nose pressed against the Plexiglas, yelling at the top of her lungs as if the rough-and-tumble atmosphere were second nature. She remembered Brian's amused then approving smile and the way he'd ceremoniously planted a garish, yellow and black Bruins stocking cap atop her head. She still had the silly hat.

After that they'd become practically inseparable. Soon Brian had acquired a drawer in her Back Bay apartment, then a closet and a key; and finally, one snowy winter day they'd shown up at City Hall and made their love legal.

McDowell made some squiggles on a pad. "I'm familiar with Brian's running career. He's been involved with Boston Road Runners for years. How about you, Ashby? How'd you get into competitive running?"

"By the back door, I'm afraid. I played field hockey in high school and in college I ran, more as a way to keep my weight down than anything else. When I met Brian, I used to accompany him to races—pit crew, that sort of thing. One day out of the blue, he challenged me to run a 10-K. He bet I wouldn't finish. That got my dander up and I accepted before I realized what I'd done. Brian ran with me, we talked. He kept my mind off the distance, and to my amazement I came in third."

"She's a natural." Brian beamed. He'd known it from the first. He still remembered the wild excitement he'd felt, like discovering a racehorse or unearthing a precious gem.

"And after that you were hooked?"

"Not quite," Ashby noted. "I thought it was beginner's luck. Brian convinced me to try another one, and mostly to prove what a fluke it was, I entered a second race. Same thing, Brian by my side, coaxing me along."

"This time second place," Brian declared proudly.

"So you began to race competitively?"

"Gradually. I discovered the exhilaration of distance running. I work with children with physical handicaps. Running became a celebration of my good fortune." She tugged at a loose strand of hair. How could she explain? She ran for the kids, the ones who could never run themselves. And she won for Brian.

McDowell reached for the tape recorder, which had resonated with a loud click and turned the cassette over. The waiter appeared with lunch and McDowell ordered another round of drinks. McDowell's easygoing air seemed to dissipate, and Ashby suspected that the hard questions were to come. Instinctively she drew a deep breath.

"So you're both gonna make a stab at the Olympics?" McDowell's eyes narrowed into a hard line. "What makes you think you can do it?"

"We think training together gives us an extra edge," Brian answered coolly. "We're good, but our secret is the support we get from each other. A lot of running is mental stamina, and that's where we have the edge— double motivation, double support."

"And your strategy is to attract attention together? America's fastest couple?" McDowell asked thickly.

Ashby winced at the double entendre.

"Exactly," Brian agreed. "We know we're the underdogs. We're not well-known, and we're fighting an uphill battle against better-known runners. You know the state of amateur road running—little support and almost no money—except for the front-runners. Training for the Olympics is full-time. We can't afford to leave our jobs, not to mention the expense of traveling to races. We need a sponsor. So, we're willing to trade financial support for product endorsement. Alone, we're just part of the hungry pack. But together we can attract attention."

"You sure proved that," McDowell grumbled. "Never seen so much publicity over a second-tier marathon."

Brian nodded. "Off the record, we picked Washington's Marine Corps Marathon for just that reason. We needed a double win, and we couldn't hope to do it in Boston or New York, not yet, anyway. The competition's too tough."

McDowell leaned back in his chair. He knotted his brows as he downed the remnants of his drink, waving to the waiter for another. "Noble intent, but a bit naive."

Brian and Ashby exchanged puzzled glances.

"Oh, you'll get the publicity and the sponsorship," McDowell agreed. "No doubt. But the question is, what will it cost you?" He lowered his voice. "Take some friendly advice. Don't do it."

Water sputtered from Ashby's lips. Had she heard correctly? Brian's furrowed brow confirmed that she had, indeed.

McDowell planted his crossed arms on the table, hunching forward as he did so. "Looks to me like you have a good thing going between you. Check around. The record book is littered with marriages that floundered on the rocks of competition." He frowned. "Better be darn sure the Olympics is worth it."

Ashby felt the color drain from her face. "You know it's a rough road, but we don't compete against each other. We're . . ."

"I know, I know." McDowell stared at the table. "It all seems so romantic now, helping each other, a common goal. The terrible truth is that reality gets in the way of romantic ideals. Everything changes when you go for the top rung."

Ashby wanted to protest, but no words came from her parched throat.

"What if only one of you makes it?" McDowell challenged. "And even if you both do—" he seemed to look inward "—competition is tough on a marriage. Make sure your goal is worth it." His tone was sober, chilling.

As if suddenly embarrassed by his words, McDowell turned his attention to the tape recorder. He rewound the cassette with more effort than it seemed to require and placed it in his pouch. "End of interview," he said in a low voice.

Ashby was glad of Brian's gift for small talk. For the rest of the meal he and McDowell talked. Ashby couldn't focus on the meaningless conversation. McDowell's unsolicited advice had thrown her out of kilter. Who had asked him to predict their future? She chided herself for letting him ruin her good mood. After all, he knew nothing about them; nothing at all about *their* marriage. She rubbed her temples, trying to exorcise her uneasiness. But a small corner of her mind kept coming back to his warning. She couldn't help wondering what lay ahead.

As if reading her thoughts, Brian reached under the table and gave her knee a reassuring squeeze. "We'll be okay," he said softly.

They skipped dessert. Even the waiter's glowing description of the chocolate mousse cake could not rouse an appetite. Finally McDowell rose from his chair. "We'll need pictures. I'll be in touch."

Ashby gave a sigh of relief as McDowell threw the strap of his satchel over one shoulder. He hesitated a moment, shifted uncomfortably, as if unsure of what to say. "Good luck to you both," he said finally, offering his hand.

They watched in silence as McDowell lumbered out the door.

"Bitter has-been," Brian muttered.

Ashby nodded. But McDowell's warning echoed through her, leaving a trace of uncertainty.

"Good luck to you both," she repeated to herself. She couldn't quite convince herself that Ted McDowell meant their running.

3

"ASHBY, we'll never get fifteen miles in, if you don't hurry." Brian's impatient voice carried up the long flight of stairs.

"Be right there, soon as I find my other shoe."

"Wear another pair."

"Got it. I'm coming."

Ashby tried to plant a cheery smile on her face as she joined Brian on the front porch of their Cambridge house, but couldn't disguise her apathy. It was getting harder and harder to keep up the onerous training schedule that Brian had devised, especially on days like today, when the sky pelted freezing rain, and the city seemed blanketed in a thick, gray cloud.

She tossed her windbreaker over her sweatshirt and stuffed the ends of her hair into the hood. "Brian, it's awful outside. Can't we skip the run?"

"We skipped it yesterday. I know it's tough, but we're barely doing the minimum. It's not as bad out as it looks," he said.

Ashby uttered a deep sigh and followed Brian into the rain. "Worse than it looks," she muttered to herself as her body reacted to the temperature with an icy shiver. Her legs seemed like lead weights as she coaxed them toward Harvard Yard. When had training become such a chore?

Their return from Washington had been wonderful. Boston had given them a hero's welcome. For a week the O'Haras reveled in their triumph. Reporters, huffing mightily, followed them on their daily runs. Fitness editors interviewed them for keeping-in-shape columns; and the newspaper's food editor featured them in a Sunday article on eating right. Ashby O'Hara's recipe for tofu lasagna, frantically borrowed from a health food freak, and Brian's premarathon pancake dinner, straight off the back of a pancake box, accompanied the article.

After the first week the media returned to covering the war in the Middle East, the famine in Africa and the scandal of a city council member indicted for bribery. Ashby and Brian went back to running quietly and unobtrusively through the neighborhood and indulging in an occasional rare steak and French fries.

Ashby breathed a sigh of relief when Ted McDowell's interview hit the stands. It was a flattering portrayal but lacked his usual zest. The story would generate interest in them, she thought gratefully, adding it to her scrapbook of press clippings.

The scrapbook was impressively thick, as was the pile of congratulatory letters, but when she and Brian came down from the high of the win and the media whirl, one terrifying problem remained. No one had offered sponsorship.

"It's only a matter of time," they comforted each other. But Ashby's optimism wore a bit thinner each day, when neither the phone nor the mail brought good news. By the month's end, Ashby could no longer summon up the cheer for even half-hearted encouragement.

"Ashby, you're slowing down! Pick up the pace!" Brian's shout brought her back to the gray day. Glancing up, she saw that Brian, stopwatch in hand, was more than his usual ten lengths ahead.

"Two minutes off!" he shouted. "Move your buns!"

"I'm going as fast as I can."

"No, you're not."

Ashby conjured up a nasty retort, but before she could get it out, Brian had turned the corner, disappearing behind a tall building. "Simon Legree," she fumed.

What's the use? she wondered. Their daily runs now seemed meaningless. Without a sponsor, the Olympics were a hopeless dream. Even Brian's Irish optimism couldn't hide that basic truth. Without money they couldn't train full-time. And anything less than an all-out effort would be futile.

She reached the footpath by the Charles River, Brian was again in sight. Ashby bristled as she noted his jaunty pace, his regular rhythm. Just like the mail, neither rain nor sleet—not even disappointment—slowed him down. His time only got better and better; hers, she had to admit, lagged sadly behind her goal. Darn him, didn't he ever get discouraged?

For Ashby every refusal, every letter of regret weighed on her shoulders like bags of sand, until it was almost impossible to move. Brian seemed unaffected by rejection. He continued to focus on technique, strategy and the next race. Was he so blind that he couldn't see it was hopeless? Washington had proved nothing. A few days of glory, a scrapbook of press clippings, but it had gotten them no further than—

"Ashby, keep your chin up, you'll run faster," Brian called over the roar of the traffic.

"And get water in my eyes?" she retorted, demonstratively wiping the drops of icy water off her brow.

"Don't worry, you won't melt."

"How do you know?"

"Take my word for it. Hey, no one ever said this would be all fun."

Fun? Not even a little fun, she muttered as she thought about the past few weeks: long days at the hospital, rushing home and running in the evenings, grabbing a meal and collapsing into bed. And on weekends they did longer runs. How she longed to sleep late just one Sunday, to have just one conversation with Brian that didn't focus on running.

"You'll never get to the Olympics, running like that." She caught sight of a yellow slicker. Brian had turned around and was jogging beside her.

Ashby stopped dead in her tracks. "What's it matter?" she cried. "We're not going, anyway. It's all over."

Green eyes peered from the yellow hood. Licks of wet hair were plastered against his forehead. Particles of ice clung to his brows. "Over? We've just begun."

"Brian, face it, we're finished."

His face creased in anger. "Can't you take a small setback?"

"You call this small?"

"Your problem is you only do your best when the press is tagging along. Can't you run without a crowd?"

"Who said anything about a crowd? But I could use just a word of encouragement every now and then. How do you think I feel having you shouting at me every step of the way? 'Ashby, do this. Not good enough!' Just who do *you* think you are?" She folded her arms defiantly at her chest, her jaw thrust out stubbornly.

His eyes blazed. "Ashby, you're a fine athlete. But unless you stop acting like a prima donna, you can forget the Olympics!"

"Well, thank you, Howard Cosell, for that astute commentary!" A tear formed in her eye and threatened to fall onto her cheek. She wouldn't give Brian the satisfaction of seeing that. She turned quickly and tore off in the opposite direction. She'd show him how fast she could run!

Out of Brian's sight she could no longer contain the tears. They streamed down her cheeks, mingling with the raindrops. She ran blindly, unaware of direction, knowing only it was away from Brian.

How dare he call her a prima donna! She trained till she was exhausted. As hard as he did. Harder. Couldn't he tell how this was tearing her up? Didn't he have feelings? She couldn't help but get discouraged. Any human would. Why, he was nothing more than a running machine—muscles, tendons and bones patched together. And no heart. Damn him. She wanted to get to the Olympics—more than he did. Only she was realistic. . . .

She felt a hand reach up and grab her collar.

"You forgot, I'm still faster." His arms wrapped around her, stopping her in midstep.

"Please, go away."

He pulled her toward him, effortlessly turned her around. From his pocket he pulled a dry bandanna, and he wiped the rain and the tears from her face. She sniffled, and he found a tissue for her nose.

"Thank you," she said stiffly.

"Ashby, don't run from me. Ever."

"I . . . I . . ."

He bent down, placing a kiss against a stubborn lower lip. His mouth was cool and moist, and he smelled like a mixture of sweat and pure rain. It was a combination she couldn't resist. His lips lingered against her stiff mouth until her resistance melted; she gave in.

He pulled away, slowly, gently. "Can I buy you a cup of coffee?"

His soft, green eyes said, "I'm sorry." She couldn't resist. It wasn't Brian she was mad at. Most runners would trade their eyeteeth for a coach this good, most women only dreamed of a husband this caring. She looked up, blinking away a few remaining tears and managed a weak smile. "Only if it comes with a muffin."

Brian looped his arm over her shoulder and drew her close, so that her head rested in the arch of his shoulder. "You're on."

ON HARVARD SQUARE, their favorite spot, the Muffin Man, was nothing more than a run-down coffee shop— Formica tables, linoleum worn bare, counters scribbled with initials of generations of Harvard students. It had been there always, outlasting most of the shops and restaurants that came and went with each faddish trend. Brian had discovered the coffee shop in his first week at Harvard. It was one of the first places he'd brought Ashby. The coffee was strong and the donuts were fresh, as was Stella, the head waitress, who barked orders at new employees, threw menus at unknowing tourists and blatantly intimidated impressionable freshmen. Those who withstood her ornery abuse became lifelong friends.

"The usual?" she asked as she seated Brian and Ashby at their favorite table. She didn't wait for an answer but just returned with two mugs of coffee and a basket of muffins.

They drank their coffee without talking, the noise of other conversations filling the silence. Brian took Ashby's hand and rubbed it softly. "I'm sorry. I was only trying to help."

"I know."

"Didn't meant to be so tough. It's just . . ." His shoulders came up in a helpless shrug.

"It's hard to keep going without some encouragement. Brian, what are our chances?"

He was silent, slicing the muffin into wedges, slathering a pat of butter onto each segment. "It's a gamble. Without money we can keep going a few months, at best. Listen, if you want to drop out, it's okay." He popped the muffin into his mouth, chewing slowly. "Maybe we should just forget it," he said finally.

Ashby felt a wave of relief sweep over her. Give it up. How she longed to return to a sane schedule, an ordinary life. She craved the luxury of spending Sunday mornings curled up with the paper, or escaping to Cape Cod for the weekend. It would be so easy, so simple to give it up. She only had to say the word. Her stomach tightened. But then she would never know if she was good enough. This was her chance. At twenty-seven she was in her prime. Who could tell what would happen in four years—injury, motherhood, career demands? She took a deep breath. It was now or never.

"I'm in." She lifted her chin. "We're not giving up."

Relief spread across Brian's taut face. "Good," he said. "I've been thinking. We thought advertisers would flock to us after one win. Instead we need to prove that we have staying power, that they need us to promote their product."

"How do we do that?"

"I think we should go to New York, make appointments with advertising agencies, anyone who'll talk to us. Go armed with our press clippings. These big companies move very slowly. Maybe they need a push. I have some friends in New York from business school who can help."

Stella appeared, refilled their mugs and dumped more oven-fresh muffins in their basket. Ashby took a bite of a buttered muffin; it melted luxuriously on her tongue. The smell of the strongly brewed coffee seemed to seep into her, filling her with a sense of warmth, of well-being. Everything would pan out. Brian would find a way.

"You really think it will work?"

"Sure." Brian returned a confident smile.

His winning smile. Brian could convince them of anything.

"It'll work." He took a long, slow sip of coffee. His jaw was clenched tight. "It'll have to," he mumbled.

ASHBY'S STOMACH TIGHTENED at the sound of a car door slamming. She couldn't wait to see Brian. The six days he'd been gone had seemed like six years. And yet she wanted to postpone the inevitable instant—that first look—when she'd know once and for all whether the New York trip had been a success. She ran to the window and peered through the darkness for the first glimpse of their car. Her heart sank as she made out the long, square lines of a neighbor's station wagon.

She checked her watch for the hundredth time. Had only three minutes gone by since she'd last looked? Brian had left New York hours ago. He'd be here any minute.

A shiver ran through her. The house felt cold and empty without Brian. The typical Cambridge colonial, white clapboard with forest-green shutters, with a wide front porch had been built at the turn of the century and added on to and renovated by each successive family. She'd immediately fallen in love with it when they'd seen it three years ago.

"Needs work," Brian had cautioned.

She had shaken her head. "Needs love."

"It's too big," Brian had pointed out.

"Good. We'll have lots of kids."

While little O'Haras hadn't materialized to fill the extra bedrooms, more often than not they had played host to a stream of runners in town for a race. Ashby loved the house best when it was filled with people.

But it was not the type of house in which to be alone. She found it depressing to eat by herself in the huge country kitchen, or worse to sleep alone in the oversize, four-poster bed that she and Brian had bought at an auction and painstakingly restored. Their bedroom, facing north, was always chilly, and neither flannel nightgowns nor a feathery comforter were adequate substitutes for Brian.

And it was not just Brian's warmth that she missed. She missed meeting for a coffee break at the hospital, catching up on the details of his work, their daily runs and his constant support. With Brian away, she fully realized how intertwined their lives had become. He was her husband, lover, best friend, coach, fellow runner, confidant and alter ego. She'd gotten so used to his presence that without him she felt maimed, as if a leg or arm were missing.

The most frustrating thing about his absence was that she was not with him, helping him. The agony of being two hundred fifty miles away, while he determined their future, was worse than she'd imagined.

In the end she'd reluctantly decided that Brian should go to New York alone because of the demands of her work. Ashby found that physical therapy was but a small part of her job. She spent a great deal of energy motivating kids to keep at their exercises. When she left town to race, her absence often played havoc with their progress, so six days in New York became unthinkable.

But while physically in Boston, her spirit was in New York. She imagined each appointment, envisioned each sumptuous lunch and dreamed of promoting everything from designer sweats to shoes.

Brian called several times, but their conversations made her uneasy. The calls were brief, sandwiched in between meetings, and Ashby had the disturbing feeling that he'd purposely timed it so he'd be unable to talk for long. She knew more about what Brian ate than what had actually been said at those meetings.

Yet his last call had been optimistic. "Looks promising," he'd told her just before leaving New York.

Ashby pulled two thick, juicy steaks and some sinfully rich éclairs from the refrigerator. Brian's homecoming warranted a celebration. Besides, cooking dinner would keep her from wearing a path to the window.

Another car. And again her stomach did flip-flops. One more trip to the window. A chill ran down her spine. Peering out, she saw Brian retrieve his suitcase. She waited for him to turn around. Her stomach tightened again. She turned away, anxious to postpone the moment of truth.

She noted the fatigue written in the bend of Brian's shoulders, as soon as he entered the house. And it was not the exhilarating kind that comes from physical exertion; rather it spoke of mental exhaustion. But his eyes gleamed and he flashed a smile. A good sign, even though on second glance she caught the tight clench of his jaw. Just fatigue, she told herself.

"How was . . . ?"

Her words were muffled as his strong arms hugged her. She nestled against his steely hardness, finding excitement in his familiarity. Her stomach unknotted just a little. He ran his fingers through her hair. Had they only been apart six days? It seemed like forever since she'd felt his fingers stroke the silky-soft strands, since she'd sensed excitement in his touch.

He loosened his grip, his lips finding hers. His mouth moved slowly over hers in a powerful kiss that was both hungry and tender.

"Babe, am I glad to be home."

"Me, too, couldn't wait."

Their eyes caught.

"So how was it?" she asked finally.

He paused for what seemed to be an eternity. "Fine." His cheerful tone sounded forced to Ashby's sharply primed ears. Nuzzling her soft neck, he added, "I'm starved. Let's talk about it over dinner."

Ashby seasoned the steak while Brian selected the wine. When he pulled the bottle of French burgundy they'd been saving for a special occasion off the wine rack, Ashby released a loud sigh.

By the time they sat down to dinner, Ashby was bursting with curiosity. "Tell me everything."

"Well you know the Big Apple, overpriced hotels, arrogant cabdrivers..."

"And?" She lifted a brow impatiently. She didn't give a damn about the scenic tour.

His fork clanked loudly on the plate. "And marketing managers, all graduates of Impress Me Academy."

"And you did?"

A sip of wine sputtered from Brian's lips.

Ashby's face drained. "What happened?"

Brian tapped the table nervously. "A lot of people were very interested—Fleet Feet, Taurus sportswear— and Sportique."

"Sportique? But that's just women's clothes. Why would they...?"

"Problem is, we're premature. Too soon to launch an Olympic campaign."

"Too soon! We're late. We should have started months ago."

"Too soon for Madison Avenue, that is. According to marketing magnates, if you start promoting the Olympics now, by the time they actually occur, the public will be saturated. Bored with the whole thing."

"But we can't wait!"

"They don't much care. Madison Avenue isn't interested in supporting amateur athletes." Brian's mouth twisted. "Only in propping up the bottom line. They're not interested in us just yet."

"When?"

Brian stared at his plate, cut off a slice of steak and popped it into his mouth. He chewed with infuriating slowness. "Everyone I spoke with was very impressed with Washington and our press clippings. And if their market research shows significant viewer recognition, and if their gurus feel that the Olympics will sell—" he gave a deep sigh "—well, in six months..."

"Six months! We can't wait. We'll be finished before we even start!" She raised her glass. "So why the special wine?"

Brian picked up the bottle and refilled their glasses, then took a long gulp. "There is one sponsor who's very interested."

Queasiness overcame her. She knew she would not like what he had to say.

"Sportique." The word hung between them.

"Brian... have they introduced a men's line?"

She knew his response even before she saw the slow shake of his head. "Only women."

She pushed the half-eaten steak away. "Then the offer... it's just for me."

His voice was flat. "Yes, only you."

"We'll tell them—"

"Ashby, just listen, please. They made a serious offer and were very generous. They think you're perfect to introduce their Luigi Sparangeti running gear."

"What does this... this... Spaghetti know about running?" Tears burned her eyes. This wasn't happening. Brian couldn't be serious.

"Brian, you know I'd never consider a sole endorsement. Why did you talk to them?"

"They came to me. Heard I was in New York looking for a sponsor. By that time I was pretty down-and-out. They're nice folks and willing to back you right away."

"What will it involve?"

"They want you to run in a series of 10-K races around the country."

"Without you?"

"That's right. The races are only women's."

Her voice was barely audible. "How long is the contract?"

"Through the Olympics."

"Is it an exclusive deal?"

He nodded.

"Then if something came through for us later, we couldn't accept it."

"That's right."

"Brian . . ."

His hand touched hers. But strangely, the warmth of his large palm did not comfort. "Ashby, it's a very generous offer. We'd have enough money to train, both of us."

"Separately."

"We'd still be running, still going for the gold."

"Alone. That's not our plan."

"I know, Babe. But it looks like it might be the only way. I think it's a very good opportunity for you."

"And for us?"

He rose from his chair. Arms folded, he turned and gazed out of the kitchen window. "I think you should consider it."

"Run without you?" Her head swam with a million thoughts. Brian was the one who made it fun. He gave her strength. The quest for the Olympics would be empty without him at her side. A lump formed in her throat. Run alone? She couldn't....

"I'd rather do it together," Brian continued. "But look at our alternatives. We can train without a sponsor and hope that something will break. And if not?" He shrugged. "Will we have the stamina to keep going alone, without the money? It's risky. Sportique's offered us a sure thing."

"Do you want me to take it?"

Slowly Brian paced the length of the kitchen. To Ashby the heavy cadence sounded like a mournful march. He did not look at her. "I told them we were interested," he said finally. "Very interested."

"I'm..."

"Ashby, let's not make a decision tonight. Please, sleep on it."

BUT SLEEP would not come. Ashby pulled the comforter up tight, but still did not feel warm. Even Brian's soft, gentle strokes, the heat of his flesh could not warm her. The chill was from within. They tossed and turned, hugged each other in quiet desperation, but curiously, like pieces of a mismatched puzzle, their bodies did not fit.

Sometime in the middle of the night, when Ashby had long ago tired of tracing the ominous shadows on the ceiling, they found release from their anxiety. Urgency replaced passion. And in the end they found physical peace, if not comfort.

Ashby turned away so that Brian did not see the tears fill her eyes. Hugging her knees to her chest, she felt truly alone, as if they'd already gone their separate ways.

Back-to-back, their bodies separated by cool distance, she did not see Brian's anguish.

4

THE FIRST HINT of the morning sun filtered through the blue-checked curtains, spilling a ray of light onto the yellow-lined page at which Brian stared. But while the new day lighted the page, Brian's thoughts remained dim and unfocused. Hours ago unable to sleep, he'd come to the kitchen, brewed a large pot of strong coffee, and, as he'd learned to do in business school when confronted with a tough decision, had taken out a fresh legal pad. At the top he'd printed Sportique, drawn a strong line down the center of the page, labeled on side Yes, the other No. The pot of coffee was almost empty, but Brian had yet to make a single entry under either heading. Was Sportique the answer, their means of achieving their Olympic dream? With a bold, black marker he drew a giant question mark on the page.

While last night he had calmly and confidently urged Ashby to accept Sportique's offer, in truth he was much less sure that it was the right decision. Sportique solved one very pressing problem, but Brian worried. Would it compromise their dream? He rubbed his forehead, remembering how the offer had come about.

He'd spent five exhausting days trekking up and down Madison Avenue from appointment to appointment. Brian had been treated politely at each stop, but in the end he had no firm offers. Discouraged and exhausted, he'd returned to his hotel—to find a message from Sportique, requesting a meeting for the next morning.

Brian arrived at Sportique well prepared and feeling confident. Claire Nash, Sportique's marketing director, had welcomed him so cordially that he hadn't given much thought to the dainty, downsize furniture into which he'd squeezed his body, or how Nash's dark eyes had glazed over when he'd discussed *his* marathon times and accomplishments. And it only dimly registered that the sketches of their new line hadn't included men's clothes.

"We're calling the collection Fashionably Fit," Nash had explained. "And we think Ashby's the perfect spokeswoman. She's exactly what we have in mind— a woman who successfully juggles career, fitness and family—in addition to looking absolutely smashing in our clothes." Nash's lips curved with satisfaction.

Suddenly it seemed to Brian as if the whole room had come into sharp focus: the obviously feminine furnishings, the sketches of women's clothes. He felt his stomach tighten at the sudden, unwanted recognition. "Ashby?" Brian struggled to admit what had finally become clear. "Your offer. It only involves her?"

Nash gave a quick smile. "I thought you understood. Our new line is for petites. Our research shows a market weakness there. No opportunity in the men's market." She waved her crimson nails. "Totally saturated."

Brian's tongue felt thick. "So...I'll have...no part."

Nash's eyes had narrowed, as if just seeing Brian for the first time, then widened with sudden inspiration. "There is some commercial potential," she said, in a way that made Brian feel as if he'd just been approved by Product Development. "In fact we might want you to accompany her to some of the races, do some interviews as the husband of Fashionably Fit Ashby O'Hara. After all, our concept here is that the Fashionably Fit woman has it all—including a wonderful husband."

"I see." Brian tugged at his tie. "Then I'm an accessory," he said, feeling inexplicably hot, "like a . . . gold watch or gym bag."

Nash laughed nervously. "I think of a supportive husband as something more."

Brian gritted his teeth. He had always blessed his good fortune in being Ashby's husband. Now, for the first time, he felt curiously diminished by that role.

But Brian had been too stunned to argue or protest. Nash had first taken his silence for interest, then shrewd negotiating, and had upped the ante, making the offer for Ashby's services more handsome than Brian had dared to hope.

But his stony silence had had nothing to do with bargaining. Once he'd absorbed the initial shock, what took its place was an emotion too raw and ugly to face: pure jealousy. Ashby was a "hot property," and he was—the husband of . . .

On the trip back to Boston, he'd been able to view Sportique's offer more rationally. His exclusion only meant that they did not sell men's clothes. Brian's mind, schooled in business, understood, but his wounded pride did not.

As Brian reflected upon those events, the wave of raw jealousy returned. Could he cope with being an also-ran? How would he feel accompanying her to races, being introduced as Ashby's husband—an attractive accessory?

And how would he really react to living off her earnings? Although Ashby had always worked full-time, Brian's salary was considerably more. He heartily endorsed woman's equality, but at his core he felt proud of his financial contributions, of his ability to support his wife. Living off Ashby? Could he handle that?

If the situation were reversed, how would Ashby feel? What if he were the one who could make their dream come true? Would she have second thoughts?

He closed his eyes and in the blackness saw an image of a giant box, wrapped in gold with a large, shiny bow. He knew what Ashby would say. If things were reversed, she would urge him to accept. She would consider it a generous gift.

Then why, he wondered, did just the thought of it make him feel so empty?

SHE'D SEEN HIM like this dozens of times, sitting at the kitchen table, his head bent, the forest-green terry cloth robe that she'd bought him their first Christmas together wrapped snugly around him. Most times she felt comforted by this familiar image of Brian, hard at work on some problem at the hospital, or devising their training schedule. But this morning the familiar did not soothe. She felt a dull ache in the pit of her stomach. Like her, Brian was wrestling with a decision and she worried. Would they both reach the same conclusion?

"Morning."

He turned with a slight start, apparently so absorbed that he hadn't heard her footsteps. "Hi, Babe." His eyes softened, but his face remained tense.

Instinctively Ashby placed her hands on his stooped shoulders, her fingers working quickly to erase his pain.

Whenever words failed or were inadequate, Ashby found that her hands spoke a soothing language.

"That feels good!" He arched his back like a content tiger and gave a deep sigh. Ashby felt a tug in her stomach; she wished it were that easy to quell her own anxiety.

"Working the night shift again?" she joked.

He nodded. "Couldn't sleep."

She leaned over his shoulder and glanced at the yellow pad, seeing Sportique boldly lettered at the top. The columns were still blank. "I see you've reached a firm decision."

He laughed. "A firm yes and a firm no." He reached up and took her hand. "I keep thinking if I stare at this long enough, something will leap out at me."

"If something leaps out at you, you know you've been at it too long." She planted a playful kiss upon his neck. "Maybe it's time to put it away for a while. How about breakfast?"

"Good idea." He pushed the pad to the center of the table, although his pensive look told Ashby it was easier to put it out of sight than out of mind.

"I think I'll make Belgian waffles."

"Hmm, haven't had that since . . ."

"We began training."

In the days before they'd made the Olympics their goal, their weekend ritual had included a huge breakfast, vast quantities of coffee and the Sunday paper. Ashby loved this languid routine. Over breakfast they had discussed everything from problems at work to when to start a family. Ashby remembered that it was over Belgian waffles, smothered in whipped cream and strawberries, that Brian had first confided his Olympic dream. And now she clutched at the symbol, hoping to find magic in the ritual.

But leisurely breakfasts, like spare time, had become one of the casualties of their quest. Their precious time was now metered into runs, weight training, swims and work.

She pulled the waffle iron from the top shelf of the kitchen cabinet, dusted it off, then hunted for the pancake mix. She found it in the back of the pantry.

"I'll make some fresh coffee," Brian offered.

She yawned. "Make it strong."

Ashby busied herself with the waffles, cracking the eggs and measuring the water with more precision than was necessary. Although she'd suggested a big breakfast, she wasn't hungry at all. She hoped that both an appetite and a decision would come.

While the waffles cooked, they discussed a friend's upcoming wedding and the latest dope on a doctor-nurse affair at work. But their half-hearted responses made it clear that the decision about Sportique occupied their thoughts. When Ashby placed the waffles on the table, she gave up any attempt at diversion.

"So what did you decide?" she asked.

Brian's face tightened, and he did not respond at once.

Ashby, waiting expectantly, added sugar to her coffee, then remembered she'd already done that.

"I guess, weighing the pros and cons," Brian said finally, "Sportique has the edge. All things considered, I think we should accept their offer."

Ashby felt her heart beat flatten. She'd thought she still had an open mind, but her involuntary response told her she'd already reached a decision. "Oh, Brian . . ."

He lifted a hand. "Please, let me finish." He wanted to get it all out, before the doubts returned, before his ego overruled good sense.

Ashby nodded glumly.

"The timing couldn't be better. We can begin training full-time—no more worries about if and when we'll get a sponsor."

Ashby pushed her plate away. "But making the Olympic team is just a part of our dream," she argued. "The other part is having a terrific time getting there and sharing the experience. When we're old and gray and can't walk—much less run—we can pull out our scrapbook and tell our grandchildren how much fun we had."

"Old and gray!" He combed a hand through his hair. "At this rate that'll happen well before the Olympics!"

Ashby knew he was joking, but his troubled eyes belied his humor. They both knew that getting to the Olympics would be demanding and grueling. The Boston Marathon in four months would be their qualifying race. If their times in that race were fast enough, they would earn the right to run in the men's and women's Olympic trial marathons a year later. There they would compete against all other U.S. qualifiers for the three slots each on the men's and women's teams. Only then, if they surmounted that last hurdle, would they be Olympians.

"If we turn down Sportique—how much longer do you think we can hold out without a sponsor?"

"A couple of months, at best."

Ashby nodded soberly. The conclusion seemed inevitable. Good sense pointed to Sportique—take the money and run—yet she stubbornly resisted. She didn't want it to be this way. She didn't want... No, it was worse than that.... *She couldn't....*

"What is it?" Brian asked. "You're white as a ghost."

"I don't want to do it alone." She lowered her eyes, avoiding Brian's knowing scrutiny.

He reached across the table, his fingers lifting her chin so that their eyes were forced to meet. "You won't be alone, I promise. I'll be with you all the way. We'll still train together. It's just that every few months you'll put on some Fashionably Fit outfit and run a 10-K race."

"Oh, Brian, you know it's not that simple."

"I'll go with you to all the races. The only difference is instead of running with you, I'll be cheering you on." He tried to be upbeat, to disguise the unwanted image that crept into his mind. Cheering her on... from the sidelines.

"It's not the same," she said softly.

There was more to it than just running the race. It started the night before. In a strange city, in a strange hotel, Brian was comfortingly familiar. When she went to bed wrapped in his arms, her body fitted snugly against his, she felt shielded. During the night Brian's strength and energy seeped into her, fortifying her. And when the race got tough, it was this cache of determination and courage that she tapped.

In the morning they would often wake early and make love. At these times their lovemaking was supercharged, as if every muscle, every fiber, every cell were alive and on edge. On these mornings his lips seared love into her flesh, his fingers singed her breasts with tenderness. And when he entered her, he filled her completely, as if her body were a soft mold waiting to receive his imprint. And at the moment of ultimate pleasure, she felt as if his life-giving fluids filled every pore, giving her new life.

Brian offered a brave smile, but she knew he, too, was conscious of all that would change. He took her hand and Ashby clung tightly, as if by holding on she could keep their dream from slipping away.

"You're right," he said. "But Sportique's a sure thing. Turn them down and we might not make it at all."

Would some other sponsor come along? Ashby didn't know. But run without Brian... Her words were barely audible. "I can't do it...alone. I can put on Sportique's fancy clothes and show up at the starting line, but without you—" she shut her eyes tight against the painful truth "—without you I won't make it to the finish line."

"What?" Brian's eyes flew open. "You don't really believe that?"

"Yes."

"In Washington I was awed by your strength. You won that race on pure courage."

She shook her head. "You don't understand. It was your courage. I couldn't let you down."

His voice was soft. "Ashby, it had nothing to do with me."

"Maybe." She stared miserably at the table.

Brian uttered a low sigh and began clearing dishes from the table.

Ashby was glad of this hiatus. She felt shaken by her own admission. How could she hope to make it to the trials, if she couldn't even face a few fun runs without him? She felt like a failure, a fraud—not an Olympic contender.

"Ashby." His tone caressed, like the fingers that ran soothingly through her hair. "Someday you'll realize just how good you are, just how capable. But I won't argue with your feelings. You're the one who will have to do the work, so it's your decision."

He took a coin from the kitchen counter and placed it in her hand. "It's your call. Heads, yes. Tails, we turn 'em down. Just remember, whichever way, I'm behind you one hundred percent."

"You're usually one hundred yards ahead," she teased, trying to ease the tense mood.

"Only in running, Babe. In everything else you're light-years ahead."

Closing her eyes, Ashby rubbed the coin between her fingers. She wished that her decision, the one in her heart, the one that would make and direct their future, was the right one.

Opening her eyes again, she carefully laid the coin on the table.

"Tails," Brian said. If he was disappointed, his voice didn't betray it.

Ashby scooped the coin off the table. "A quarter says something better will come along."

Brian laughed. "You're willing to wager the whole thing?"

"All of it."

But as Brian pocketed the quarter, her smile faded. Ashby knew that she'd just staked far more. Riding on that slim coin were their hopes and their dreams.

ASHBY COLLAPSED into the armchair and faced her friend and physician Gina DuShea across the desk. Gina, with her soft, coppery hair, her ample curves and her heart-shaped face, looked like a heroine from a plantation novel. She'd grown up in New Orleans, and her graceful, unhurried movements, her soft, Southern accent, presented a refreshing contrast to the rushed atmosphere of the hospital. Gina never seemed too busy for patients or friends.

Gina had listened intently as Ashby described her symptoms—a persistent cold and cough, trouble sleeping and fatigue. She'd taken Ashby's vital signs, probed her throat, nose, chest and recorded her weight. She'd taken a blood test to check her iron level.

"Give it to me straight, Doc," Ashby joked, when Gina concluded the examination. "How long to live?"

"Honey, unless you take it easy for a bit, I advise you to get your will in order."

Ashby's jaw tensed. "That bad?"

"Frankly you're thin as a rail and exhausted. Right now you've got nothing more than a pesky cold, nothing that a week of R and R and TLC won't cure. I'd admit you to the hospital, if I thought you'd rest there. If you don't slow down, you'll never get rid of it."

Ashby threw her hands into the air. "I'm eating three square meals and getting plenty of exercise."

"It's the plenty of exercise that concerns me. Just how much?"

"Much less than we should be getting. We're barely running eighty miles a week. I'm trying to lift weights at lunch...."

"Please!" Gina raised a hand. "I'm tired, just listening. How much longer are you planning to keep up this idiotic pace?"

Ashby shrugged. "Not much longer," she said with more hope than certainty. "Brian thinks something will break any minute now."

Ashby tried to sound confident, but in truth she was worried. When she'd boldly turned down Sportique's offer, she'd gambled that there'd be a better offer for both of them. But weeks later there was still nothing. Still too early to commit, the corporations claimed. As the Boston Marathon—their crucial qualifying race— came closer, she knew that they were approaching a deadline. If they didn't find a way to train full-time within the next few weeks, they'd have to give up their Olympic dream.

"You keep this up for much longer, and the only thing you'll be running is a chronic fever. You're on the brink of collapse. And frankly, so's Brian. I'm not the only one who's noticed him sleeping through staff meetings," Gina said.

"I know." Ashby had also seen him nod off during their interminable administrative sessions. His fatigue was so palpable that she could feel it. Despite his solid muscles he looked gaunt and spare. And at night they curled their aching, weary bodies around each other and slept like babies, unapologetically. Their passions had given way to exhaustion. They'd become too tired for love.

"Look, honey, before you both get desperately ill, ask yourself, is this thing really worth it?"

"I have. And I've decided it is. We'll never have another opportunity. In another four years—" she shrugged "—who knows? Besides, we'd like to have a family."

"Then there must be another way to do it, short of killing yourself. Have you considered your family? Surely your mother would help."

Ashby stiffened. "I could never ask her."

"Why not?"

"She disapproves. She thinks I should be volunteering for the Daughters of the American Revolution, not running."

"Have you asked her?"

"No. On top of all the other rejections, I'm not sure I could handle hers, too."

Gina nodded sympathetically. "But maybe she'll surprise you. You could appeal to her patriotism. By supporting you, she'd be making a major contribution to the American Olympic effort."

Ashby cradled her head between her hands. "I dread asking her."

Gina's eyes lighted with a sudden inspiration. "Maybe I can help." She reached into her desk drawer, pulled out a pad and scribbled madly. "Here," she said, handing Ashby the prescription. "Think of it as following doctor's orders."

Ashby laughed as she read what Gina had written. "RX," it said. "Ask your mother! ASAP."

5

BRIAN FIDGETED nervously with his tie as he sat on the velvet settee in the parlour of Ashby's mother's house. "How do I look?"

Ashby's eyes widened in appreciation as they strayed over his dove-gray suit, his starchy oxford shirt and his foulard tie, then slid down the pressed creases of his trousers. "Hmm, good enough to take home."

"How about good enough to take home to Mother?"

"Irresistible! You'll have Mother eating out of your hand."

"Your mother," he whispered nervously, "only eats off of fine china."

Ashby squeezed his knee. "Don't worry, this will go just fine."

But despite Ashby's assurances, Brian was unconvinced. He hadn't approved of Ashby's plan to ask her mother for a loan. Only when it became clear that Ashby intended to ask without Brian's approval had he reluctantly lent his support.

"I was the one who decided to turn down Sportique," Ashby had argued, "and so it's up to me to find another way."

"But your mother," Brian had protested. "We agreed we'd never ask her. After what happened in Lexington, how could you even think of it?"

Ashby had flinched at the mention of Lexington. "I know, I swore I'd never ask her...but given the circumstances, I'm willing to forget."

"And forgive?"

Ashby had nodded slowly, sadly. "I'm willing to let bygones be bygones. Besides, that was all before..." Her palms had turned upward. Before their choices had run out, she thought.

Now as Brian's eyes wandered around the imposing parlor, the windows draped in thick velvet, the heirloom Oriental rugs, his discomfort returned. He wished desperately he'd talked Ashby out of this. He jammed his hands into his pockets helplessly. If only he'd turned up something else.

"Are you sure you want to go ahead with this?" he asked one last time.

"I'm sure." Her damp hand stroked the arm of the velvet settee. "Besides," she added, trying to brush off her own anxiety, "the way I figure it, our only hopes are the lottery, a bake sale or my mother. I've never won anything in my life, I've never baked a cake, so that leaves my mother."

"Do you know how much pride we'll have to swallow to ask your mother for money? It's humiliating." He bowed his head, as if she'd already turned them down.

"Darlings!" Elizabeth Clayton fluttered into the parlor.

In many ways Ashby was a copy of her mother. Ashby had inherited Elizabeth's petite frame, her deep sapphire eyes, her heart-shaped face and her assurance. Brian marveled at how those similarities could hide such differences. Elizabeth was bound by convention and tradition, and Ashby cared nothing for them.

Elizabeth was wearing a deep violet dress, and with her hair piled crownlike atop her head, Brian thought she looked imperial. He wondered if Ashby would someday look that way, too.

Elizabeth took his hand and brushed his cheeks with her lips, then lightly kissed the air between Ashby and herself. "So glad you could come to dinner. Ashby tells me she had something very important to discuss. I can't wait to hear about it."

In spite of Elizabeth's professed interest, conversation drifted to everything but Ashby's news. As they sat in the high-backed mahogany chairs and made their way through course after course, Brian wondered if they'd ever get to the purpose of their visit. Over soup they discussed the exhibit of German Masters at the Museum of Fine Arts; over the fish course an upcoming family wedding. With the main course, ragout of lamb, Elizabeth served up a discussion of the coming opera season.

As dessert approached, Brain's eyes flashed a "What's up?" But he couldn't decipher the tiny nod that Ashby returned. Relief vied with apprehension. Had she changed her mind? Or was the dreaded discussion still to come?

"I hope that you'll be coming to the Heart Ball this year," Elizabeth said as dessert was served. "You missed it last year and the year before, and I did promise Mrs. Eldridge that you'd attend this year."

"When is it?" Ashby asked, sighing.

"Patriot's Day—same as every year."

Brian's fork froze midway to his mouth. Suddenly the German chocolate cake lost its appeal.

"But, Mother, that's the Boston Marathon."

"Dear, couldn't you skip it just once?"

"Not this year." Ashby stomach knotted. Brian's impassive expression told her she was on her own. Ashby faced her mother. "Boston is our qualifying race for the Olympic trials."

Elizabeth waved her hands in dismissal. "I've never understood this running thing. Frankly, I'd hoped you'd gotten over it."

"Over it? Mother, we've just started."

Elizabeth looked surprised. "You hadn't mentioned it."

Ashby hadn't talked about it. Running had become a topic she'd avoided with her mother—ever since Lexington.

It was a 20-K run in the fall through the historic towns of Lexington and Concord. Ashby always looked forward to the race; the foliage was at its peak, and so it became a celebration of autumn. Ashby hoped that her mother would be moved by the beauty and somehow come to understand Ashby's love for running.

Spurred on in part by her mother's presence, Ashby had been the first woman to finish. When she won, she felt a schoolchild's delight at pleasing her mother. On the victory stand Ashby had scoured the crowd, searching face after face for Elizabeth. But she'd been unable to pick her out. "Mother," she'd called, lifting the trophy above her head. "Will you join me up here?"

The crowd's eager buzz faded as those present waited, first expectantly and then impatiently.

"Mother," Ashby called again. But the only response was silence.

Ashby wasn't sure how long she'd stood there, her body turning red with embarrassment, her eyes flooding with humiliation. But she knew that she'd never felt more abandoned than when she realized her mother had gone home.

Trying to recover, Ashby had smiled bravely, but the trophy hanging limply in her hand suddenly felt worthless. Brian had rushed onto the stage, encircling her in a warm, proud hug. But even Brian's crucial love couldn't compensate for that primal pain.

Elizabeth had never explained her sudden disappearance, and Ashby had been too hurt to ask. She'd resolved never to leave herself vulnerable to her mother again. Until now.

"We're still aiming for the Olympics," Ashby said, jutting her chin with determination.

"I can't think why you like it," Elizabeth mused, "the dirt, the sweat, the injuries." Her voice trailed off to a thin whisper. "The pain."

For a second Ashby was taken aback by how vulnerable her mother looked.

"I was hoping by this time there'd be grandchildren."

Under the table Ashby felt Brian touch her knee.

"There'll be plenty of time for grandchildren," Ashby promised, "after the Olympics."

Her mother shrugged. "I've always wished your father had lived long enough for grandchildren." Her voice seemed to drift away as she gazed at the stern portrait of Ashby's father, Gordon, above the mantle. "And I'm not getting any younger."

Her mother's jab hit home. Kids. It was something that Brian and she had talked about. Ashby was certain that their decision to delay the start of their family was the right one for them.

But sometimes it seemed as if her biological yearnings would sabotage her resolve. Inexplicably her breasts grew tender whenever she cradled a newborn in her arms. And those times she secretly questioned the wisdom of delaying one dream for another, one which was as elusive as the wind.

She gazed up into Brian's eyes and saw her concerns mirrored there.

"We hope to make you a proud grandmother many times over," Brian told Elizabeth. "And we hope you'll be just as proud of us when we make the Olympic team."

Ashby was grateful for Brian's intervention; she felt the tension ease just a little bit. But her relief was only momentary. When she glanced back at her mother, Elizabeth's back was stiffly straight, a brow imperiously arched. "*If* you make the team," Elizabeth said sharply.

Brian saw the color drain from Ashby's face, her eyes fill with pain. He grasped the edge of the table, trying to contain his ire.

For what seemed like an eternity they ate in stony silence. Only the occasional chime of silver against porcelain broke the grim hush.

Ashby glanced at the portrait of her father and felt an old ache. He'd died when she was in college, but she still missed him—especially at times like this. His love had been so easy, so unequivocal, her mother's so much harder to earn.

"I've had a letter from Aunt Lydia," Elizabeth said, when the silence had become unbearable. "Lots of rain in Palm Beach."

"Is that so?" Brian smiled with relief, grateful for the reprieve and anxious to discuss anything but their running. He tossed a safety net to Ashby. "Isn't that strange for this time of year?" But she refused to be saved.

Instead she met her mother's eyes. Taking a deep breath, she fought her impulse to accept Brian's rescue, to simply give up. "Mother, we did want to talk about the Olympics." Again Ashby looked to Brian for support. But his eyes only flashed a warning.

Ignoring it, Ashby plunged on. "In fact, what we wanted to ask you—Ouch!" She recoiled from a swift blow to her leg.

"What we wanted to ask," Brian interrupted, turning his back to Ashby, "is whether you think golf should be an Olympic sport?"

"HOW COULD YOU?" They were at the car, icy rain was pelting down, and Ashby's anger, which had simmered through the rest of dinner, spewed forth like steam from an overheated radiator.

"Why?" she demanded. Her angry words became hot vapors and rose in the space between them. "We agreed that I'd ask for a loan."

Brian stared at the sidewalk. "I'm sorry. I couldn't take it. The way she feels about our running." He shrugged. "I couldn't take her money."

The way Elizabeth Clayton had swiftly disarmed them with a simple "if" had overwhelmed him. As Ashby's face fell his own impotence had been transformed into anger. And then a more urgent emotion had taken over: a wild, primitive need to protect, to shield Ashby from her mother. He'd done it clumsily, in a way that had hurt Ashby. But in that instant he hadn't cared about money, about running. He hadn't given a damn about the Olympics. Nothing, nothing at all was worth seeing Ashby hurt.

"I was only asking for a loan."

"I don't care. Tainted money. It would cloud everything. Every dollar would remind me of her disapproval. I couldn't do it." *I couldn't let her hurt you like that.* He kicked the sidewalk. "I'd rather rob a bank."

"That's twenty years in prison!"

"Hers would be a life sentence. If we made the team, we'd be forever beholden, and if we didn't—" he waved his hands helplessly "—we would never hear the end. It would be a debt we'd never repay."

"Well, we don't have to worry about that now!" She pivoted, her hair pulling lose from its neat French knot. Yanking the car door open, she dropped into the seat and slammed the door.

Brian climbed into the driver's seat. He glanced at Ashby, an apology on his lips, but the look on her face said, "Don't even try." He turned away.

Ashby pulled up the collar of her coat as if to insulate herself, to create a wall against her mother, against Brian. She was furious at them both: at her mother's rigid, proper world that had no room for her, and at Brian, who had promised his support, then undermined her. His big, male ego. Couldn't he swallow his pride just long enough to let her ask? Would it have really been a mortal wound to accept the loan? She'd be damned if she'd let his pride get in the way of her dream!

Brian was driving with a hand on the horn, his foot on the gas pedal. Damn them all—Elizabeth and the corporations. He'd had it with them all. Too risky! Not the right time! Not good enough! He blasted a motorist whose only crime was lingering a little too long at the light. He'd known their quest would be physically tough, but he hadn't realized what the emotional toll would be. No one had warned him about the waiting, the begging, the endless rejections, the hurt and humiliation. it was hard enough on him, but he hated what it was doing to Ashby. Now, for no reason, his fist rammed the horn.

Running together, going after a dream had seemed so romantic. He hadn't known it would also be lonely. He'd thought family, friends, sponsors would rally to their support. But it was just the two of them. Alone. Damn, didn't anyone believe in them?

Ashby grabbed the overhead strap as Brian screeched into a turn. Maniac! Glancing up, she realized she had no idea of where they were. Certainly not heading toward Cambridge, as they should be. They were downtown, just passing the Common.

Her spine stiffened. "Brian, where are you taking me?"

"You'll see." His gritty tone said, "Don't ask."

They passed the Boston Gardens. She wanted to go home, to crawl into bed, to sleep, to forget. She had no interest in riding to . . .

Abruptly Brian stopped the car, the gears whining into reverse as he maneuvered it into a parking space.

"Where in the world . . . ?"

He reached over and flung her door open. "We're going for a walk."

Icy sleet clouded the windshield. "Now? In this?"

"Yes."

"Have you gone mad?"

"Mad?" He scowled. "Very mad."

He was walking briskly up the block, and she had no choice but to join him. A gale of wind rushed through the corridor of tall buildings, sending a shiver down her spine. She quickened her pace. But she was wearing heels, not her running shoes. She tottered, twisting her ankle. A truck tore down the street, sending sheets of water splattering in her direction. Cold mud washed down her legs. "You fool!" she yelled at both Brian and the truck driver. "Would you please wait!"

Brian stopped and turned.

Fuming, Ashby marched up the hill. She caught up to him at the corner. "Why are we tearing up—"

Then she saw it. At her feet were the faint remnants of a yellow line.

It looked so different now. The tall spires of Trinity Church were lost in the fog, distorting the familiar scene.

She had never actually walked this before. She had always hit the street running, a stream of spectators lining the path, cheering her on as her feet slapped the pavement in a last, desperate surge to the finish line.

Brian was standing under a streetlight, staring at the sheer, glass facade of the Hancock Tower, symbol of the Boston Marathon, signal of the race's end.

The wind had picked up, whipping Brian's trench coat about like a kite. His hair was blowing, and rain streaked his face. But he seemed oblivious to it all, as if he'd withdrawn into himself.

Ashby stood at some distance, watching, waiting. Then suddenly his face eased, and he smiled as if he'd suddenly solved some complex riddle. She moved to his side and stared at the building, as if she, too, would find some answer. But she saw just row after row of glass. "Brian," she asked finally, "why are we here?"

He took her hand and gestured toward the yellow line. "It's the end," he said, his voice calm and sure. "And the beginning."

"The beginning?" she repeated.

"*Our* beginning." Releasing her hand, he bent down and traced the line. "I needed to see it, to feel it, to make sure our dream was real. And now I know we can do it. Babe—" he looked up, his eyes filled with determination "—we can do it by ourselves."

He stood and Ashby thought that he'd never looked so tall, so resolute, so strong. He pulled her so close that she could feel the heat from his breath, so that his determination became hers. His hand closed tightly around hers, then lifted, and their arms formed a triumphal arch.

"On Patriot's Day we're gonna fly across this line on our way to the Olympics. Nothing will stop us. No one. We're unbeatable. Ashby, we've got all it takes."

Their lips met and Ashby knew he was seeing more than reconciliation. The kiss was more than an apology. His lips burned into hers, sealing a promise. It bound them inexorably to each other.

They came together, her breasts crushed against his chest, his body sheltering her, hers warming him until they were one: an invincible force.

"Just us," Brian whispered, as their lips finally parted.

Ashby ran a finger against his lips, still moist with her kiss. She tossed her head back and laughed in recognition, with pleasure. The fog had lifted around the spires of Trinity Church, and it was all suddenly brilliantly clear.

"Just you and me." She snuggled tightly against him, remembering something she'd really known all along. "Us," she said, squeezing his hand tight. "It's all we need."

6

THE WHITE-HAIRED JEWELER was busy with a customer, so Ashby waited patiently, happy to spend a few minutes admiring the cases of antique estate jewelry, the shop's specialty.

Their third wedding anniversary was ten days away, and she'd yet to settle on a gift for Brian. Her eyes drifted from cuff links to gold buttons and pocket watches, lingering on a particularly beautiful watch, until Ashby calculated how many pairs of running shoes she could buy instead.

Ashby's mother had pointed out that third anniversaries were insignificant—marked by a gift of crystal or leather. But Ashby refused to accept her mother's pronouncement. This year had been especially important. Their decision to try for the Olympics had created a special bond—a shared goal. Next year, together, they would fulfill their dream.

In the past few weeks Ashby had felt particularly close to Brian, immensely proud to be his wife. Ashby didn't believe in magic moments, personal or divine, but despite that, she strongly felt that the evening— some three weeks ago—when they'd stood together at the foot of the Hancock Tower, had marked a significant turnabout. She felt revitalized, surer than ever of their commitment to each other, of their ability to see their dream come true, no matter what.

"May I help you?"

She looked into a face as antique as the jewelry. "Is there anything you'd like to see?"

She shook her head. "Not today, I'm afraid. But I have some jewelry I'd like appraised for insurance." Her neighbor's house had been burglarized in broad daylight, scaring Ashby, and she'd promised Brian to keep the doors locked, even when she was at home.

The jeweler gave her a knowing smile. "Let's see."

She pulled a velvet pouch from her handbag. The old man sifted through the pieces: an opal ring, gold earrings, a carved cameo. His flat, gray eyes flashed with excitement when he took out the sapphire pendant.

Ashby was pleased by his obvious interest. He had selected the piece of jewelry she loved: a pear-cut sapphire surrounded by a sea of diamond chips. The contrast between the regal deep blue and the glittery diamonds was what gave the piece its drama.

"Now this is something special." He placed his jeweler's loupe in his left eye, moving the magnifying lens close as he examined the stones. "This sapphire is one of the finest I've seen." He looked up and smiled again. "It's exactly the same shade as your eyes."

Ashby grinned. "I know."

He turned the piece over and peered through the loupe once more. "There's a jeweler's mark." He pressed the glass against it. "Hawthorne, late eighteenth century, one of England's finest craftsmen. It's very valuable," he explained. "How did you come to own it?"

"It's been in my family for generations, passed down to the oldest daughter."

On her sixteenth birthday her family had celebrated with a dance. Ashby had felt especially grown-up. For the first time she'd worn a long dress, one of the palest lilac, with wispy spaghetti straps and stays in the bra that gave her a figure she'd only dreamed of.

Ashby remembered the bittersweet look on her father's face as she'd tottered into the parlor on a pair of high heels. "Suzanne, you're no longer..." He had smiled, though his eyes were damp as he kissed her cheek. "You're a woman."

Her mother's scrutiny had been more critical. She'd fussed with Ashby's hair, retying the long bow in the back of her gown, and admonished Ashby about her posture. "Shoulders back."

Needing her mother's reassurance, she'd asked, "Mother, do I look okay?"

"Almost perfect."

Ashby had been crestfallen; predictably, she hadn't lived up to her mother's exacting standards.

But as the corners of her mouth turned down, her mother had unfastened the sapphire pendant from her own throat. "You know about the pendant, Suzanne. Today it's yours." She proudly fastened it around her daughter's neck.

Gordon had looked on, beaming. "It was meant for you. Sapphire eyes like your mother's."

The jeweler now ran his callused fingers along the gold rim. "Do you have any interest in selling?" he asked hopefully.

She shook her head. "I wouldn't want it to pass out of the family."

Ashby didn't care very much for jewelry, but she loved the pendant. As an awkward adolescent, never feeling quite right, never quite fitting in, the pendant had always made her feel special.

And she'd never tired of the story—family folk-lore—about her aunt Amanda, the pendant's original owner, nor of her mother's insistence that sapphire-blue eyes were always inherited by the eldest daughter, along with the pendant. Ashby thought about the unbroken tradition, and how she would proudly continue it. "Someday," she told the jeweler, "it will go to my daughter."

The craftsman nodded and smiled. "I understand. I have daughters of my own." With evident regret he returned the piece to Ashby. "Then I'll just fill out the appraiser's form."

"Thanks." The pendant was beautiful, she thought, as she impulsively put it on and recalled again the occasions when she'd worn it—for the senior prom, as the "something blue" at her wedding. And as she glanced into the mirror, thoughts of tradition and celebration swelled her heart.

"By the way," she asked as her thumb stroked the gold edge. "How much do you think the pendant's worth?"

She was sure she must have heard wrong. "Excuse me?" Her jaw dropped, and she had to ask the jeweler to repeat the amount.

He did: the same figure. She tightened her grip on the pendant—irreplaceable and valued beyond money.

She blinked in disbelief. "That's almost enough... Are you sure?"

The old jeweler nodded slowly, solemnly.

A LIGHT SNOW was falling as Brian placed two small suitcases in the trunk of the car. "Gobs of room in here," he said, surveying the half-full trunk and the few bags of groceries in the back seat. "Are you sure this is all we need?"

"Positive," Ashby said. "The cabin's fully equipped."

Brian narrowed his eyes as he examined the empty ski rack. "Maybe we should take the skis, just in case."

She shook her head resolutely. "No skis."

"The snowshoes?"

"Absolutely not."

"A winter weekend in Vermont without them? It doesn't feel right."

"Trust me. It'll be just fine."

"We won't get bored?"

She grinned. "Not a chance."

"What will we do?"

She laughed. "Absolutely nothing. That's the whole idea. No running, no skiing, no housework, no worries about the hospital. Just the two of us, remember?"

"Yeah, I know. It's just that it's been so long. I think I've forgotten how to do nothing."

Ashby wrapped a hand around his waist and pulled him close. "It's like riding a bike, it comes right back. And if not . . . I'll remind you." Her voice, playfully seductive, hinted at what the lessons might be.

"You think I'm trainable?" He pressed his hand against the back pockets of her jeans.

"I'm counting on it."

Their easy banter, Ashby thought, hid a hard truth. Their schedules had been so frenzied that doing nothing was a foreign concept.

She had a very special purpose for this weekend in the woods of Vermont. Their grueling schedule had left little time or energy for love. More often than not,

lovemaking was sandwiched into a few spare minutes
or sacrificed for a good night's sleep.

Ashby feared that as the competition grew more
heated, their passions would cool still further. Being
alone together would give them a chance to reignite the
flames of passion that had once been the best part of
their relationship.

"Ashby, going to the cabin is the nicest anniversary
present."

"I'm glad you like it."

Ashby thought about the gold watch she'd seen in the
jewelry store, about the clothes and books she'd almost bought, until it had dawned on her that the most
precious gift they could give each other was themselves.

They'd spent their honeymoon in Dan's cabin in
Vermont. It had gotten their marriage off to a perfect
start. She savored the memory of that languid weekend whenever their hectic routine made her feel most
distant from Brian.

"Like it! It's inspired."

"Just wait till you see what I have planned for tonight." She fluttered her lashes.

Brian grinned. "Let's get started. I don't want to miss
out." He felt in his pocket for the cabin keys. "Got
everything?"

Ashby wiped the foggy window with her gloved
hands and peered inside, searching among the brown
bags in the back seat for one in particular. "Yes," she
said when she spotted that bag.

Brian slipped his hand into his jacket pocket, checking for a small box. He smiled as his fingers found it.

"So," he said as they climbed into the front seat, "we're on our way."

But it seemed as if they might never get there. Vehicles were bumper-to-bumper, and an accident slowed them on the interstate. Ashby could feel Brian's exasperation mount as he negotiated the stop-and-go traffic.

When they finally got off the interstate, the snow thickened, the flakes clotting against the window like frothy cream. But curiously they both seemed to relax. Fresh snow coated the bare branches of birch trees, transforming the farms into Norman Rockwell landscapes.

"With a little luck—" Brian grinned "—we'll be snowed in."

Ashby rested her head lightly on his shoulder, and a slow smile lighted her face. "My fantasy, too."

He turned, their eyes met and the car suddenly seemed damp, overheated. His tongue circled his dry lips, which seemed to taste of Ashby. "Like the last time," he said quietly.

She nodded almost imperceptibly.

As they climbed into the mountains, the visibility decreased to just a few feet. Ashby noticed how the snow did more than limit their vision, it narrowed their view of the world to the here and now. Their worries and concerns about their future seemed to dissolve like the snowflakes against the heated windshield. She reached up and stroked Brian's cheek and felt an impatient surge of desire.

The heat from their bodies made the air cloyingly close, trapping the scent of Ashby's light cologne. The scent reminded Brian of how her hair smelled just after it was washed, of her naked body atop fresh sheets, of the fragrance that lingered in the hollow of her throat. The tick of the windshield wiper became a metronome, measuring out impatient seconds.

"Are we almost there?" she asked, sensing his impatience.

"Maybe fifteen miles."

"I can hardly wait."

He slipped his hand into hers and gave it a tight squeeze. "Me neither."

THE CABIN was cold and dark. Using a flashlight Ashby scrounged around until she located the oil lanterns. She lighted them quickly and the amber flames emitted a shadowy light.

The A-frame cabin was much as she remembered, really one room, with a huge wood stove used for heating and cooking in the center. The floor was of varnished pine, and a thick fur rug sat in front of the stove. There were several armchairs made of rough timber, a small table, and in the corner a sink, an ice chest and some open shelves. A wooden ladder led to a sleeping loft, but they preferred to sleep by the fire, wrapped in quilts.

Ashby opened the shades that covered a wall of glass. Icicles hung from the window like a glittery valance. There was no one else around; the only other light came from the moon and stars.

"Brian, I love it here. It's perfect."

"I know. Why did we wait so long to come back?"

She took his hand. "Let's make this an annual event."

They didn't talk much as they set to work, making the cabin home. Brian took charge of the wood-burning stove, feeding it first small kindling, then gradually adding spruce, pine, hickory and oak logs. Soon the woodsy fragrance permeated the small space.

Then Ashby emptied cans of soup into a pot and set it atop the stove along with some thick-crusted bread. She unwrapped some creamy brie and placed it near the fire to melt it slowly. They had dinner on the rug, warmed by the fire from the stove, and Ashby couldn't remember when anything had tasted so good.

Brian climbed into the loft and brought down quilts and blankets.

Ashby smiled. "Just like our honeymoon. Three days, and we didn't even go outside."

Brian grinned. "We're old married folks now and besides, we only have two days."

Ashby's mouth curved with pleasure as she remembered those three days—a honeymoon that had been as spontaneous as their wedding.

A blizzard, enormous even by Boston standards, had paralyzed the city and closed the hospital. They had been thrilled by the forced holiday. They played games: Monopoly, poker, backgammon. They listened to nostalgic love songs and danced close. They made love at odd hours.

The next morning it was still snowing. Wrapped tightly in Brian's arms, Ashby had woken with a profound sense of contentment. She had never felt so loved, so protected.

Brian had woken, slowly. "Let's get married," he had proposed, an eye barely opened, a smile parting his lips.

"A proposal?"

He'd nodded and pulled her still closer, so that she felt the heat of his breath, the desire in his body.

Brian had glanced at the windows fogged by ice. "I'd get down on my knees and do this properly, if it weren't so cold." He pulled the comforter up and wrapped it around them like a cocoon.

"Knees or not, I accept. When?" she had asked, somehow not surprised that his proposal had come at this time, in this way.

"Today."

She laughed. "Don't we need announcements, guests, caterers . . . ?" His lips found hers, moist, urgent, calming. And suddenly she'd known that none of those things was important.

He shrugged. "Just someone to marry us."

"But we'll never find anyone in the middle of a blizzard."

But they did. They called City Hall and found that one judge—in traffic court—had indeed made it through the storm. Then they commandeered Dan and Gina as witnesses. Gina, a traditionalist, had rustled up something old, new and borrowed. Dan, as best man, had offered his class ring as proxy, until a suitable wedding ring could be purchased.

After a short ceremony in the chambers of the traffic court judge, the four had trudged through snowdrifts to Donatello Ristorante, their favorite North End restaurant. Sometime after they had devoured copious quantities of pasta, veal and fish, Dan had produced the keys to his cabin. "What's a wedding without a honeymoon?" he'd inquired. As soon as the roads were cleared, they'd headed for Vermont.

Ashby remembered how she'd grown nervous on that first drive to the cabin. Although she'd known Brian for more than a year, she suddenly felt as if she didn't know him at all. A lifetime together? It seemed a bold gamble in a world where marriages were tossed aside like worn-out running shoes. What made them think they were stronger, smarter, luckier or more in love than the others?

Their love had held a special flavor during those days. Their passion was tinged with tenderness, as if the marriage ceremony itself had sobered them, made them aware how precarious love was.

"I can't believe it's been three years," she said, her mind paging through her mental scrapbook, savoring each memory, thinking how their love had flowered, grown stronger.

Brian gave her a bittersweet smile. "Time sure flies."

Too quickly, she thought, her eyes darkening. "I wish we could slow it down."

"Let's try," he said as his lips met hers in a soft, aching kiss that lingered against her mouth—moist, sweet and minty. As his lips nibbled, as his tongue roamed the deep recesses of her mouth, she remembered the dizzying delights of just a kiss. When he pulled his lips away, she could not tell if mere seconds, or perhaps minutes had passed.

Ashby uttered a low sigh of satisfaction. Just as he'd promised, they'd slowed down time—captured a few precious minutes and preserved them as if between glass—to be remembered and cherished forever.

The cabin was warming, filling with the woodsy aroma of the burning wood, the smell of smoldering pine needles. The glow of the fire and its earthy scents filled her with a sense of well-being that she hadn't felt in months. Brian felt it, too, she could tell. The deep lines on his forehead had eased; his jaw had relaxed, and his lips had curved into an easy smile she'd almost forgotten.

"Slow enough?" he asked as his fingers twisted one, then another of the buttons on her jersey until all twelve were free. He pulled the jersey over her head.

"Not quite," she teased as she took his hand and placed a finger in her mouth, sliding her tongue down one finger and up the next. His callused fingertips felt like sandpaper.

Brian groaned with disappointment when she placed the last finger in her mouth, twisting her tongue so that it curled around it and made soft, sucking sounds. A smile spread slowly across his face. "The other hand," he said, his eyes soft with desire.

She obliged, then took his moist hands and pressed them against her breasts, where his slippery fingers moved in sultry circles against the curved mounds. He cupped her breast, then gently rubbed her taut nipples between his fingers.

She shimmied his shirt over his head, brushing his torso with her hands, delighting in the contrasts—the bristly feel of his chest, the baby-smooth skin down his sides, the weathered texture of his back, and finally, most delightfully, the hidden silk of his neck.

"Hmm, your hands feel like angels' wings." He captured her hands and wrapped them in his, bringing them to his lips.

They wrestled out of their jeans, Ashby tugging at Brian's cuffs as he wriggled and danced free. At last they lay side by side, their bare, damp bodies glowing in the heat of the fire. Now they did not touch, instead they let their eyes savor, explore and entice.

Ashby's breathing grew tight as she saw Brian's hot gaze move along the soft swells of her body, his mouth curling with pleasure, his eyes softening as they passed from curve to curve. In turn, her eyes ravaged the planes of his body, his lean, taut muscles. She felt her heart pound with urgency, her fingers tingle with desire.

But still they did not rush; they reveled in the luxury of time and used it lavishly. She ran her fingers through his hair, traced the planes of his face, moving by memory to the thick scar on his chin, then once more to his mouth that was open and waiting. Had she ever noticed before the splash of freckles on his cheeks that looked like a comet's tail, or the whiteness of his eyelids?

His lips strayed down her palm, her arms, her neck, then to her breasts. His tongue felt like superfine sugar as it stroked her sensitive flesh, then inched lower across her abdomen, her navel, her sensitive tummy, around her hips. His palms pressed deeply into her buttocks, and Ashby arched with unabashed desire.

His tongue left a moist trail as it moved to her inner thighs, lashing with catlike licks. He lingered at those caches of desire, the tip of his tongue etching exquisite pleasure as his hands crushed her soft, pliant bottom.

Her soft purrs deepened as pleasure spread through her like a hot, languid wave; she gripped him tightly as the waves filled her, flooded her.

"Touch me," he asked urgently, guiding her to where his maleness burned like slow coals. Her fingers stroked, her mouth caressed, her tongue lashed. And when she sensed that his white heat would soon explode, she guided him, so that their bodies came together at long last.

Their tempo was no longer slow and tempting, but wild and urgent. They moved against each other, each stroke mirrored in the other, like perfectly practiced partners in a tortured tango. Finally Brian's body thundered against Ashby, and as the heat of his passion coursed through her, she rocketed with the force of a thousand shooting stars. The blazing furies set her free, and at the same time bound her inevitably, inextricably to Brian.

Moments later they lay coiled around each other, her head cradled in the crook of his arm, his legs tossed over her hips, their arms braided so that it was impossible to tell where she began and he ended. Their breathing slowed to the same, soft melody, their hearts became muffled drums, beating a rhythm of contentment.

Ashby loved these first, unguarded moments after love, when defenses were stripped bare. She lazily traced the line of sweat running down Brian's torso. Ashby thought she'd never felt closer. She clung tightly to Brian, as if by doing so she could hold onto these precious moments.

"You okay?" he asked.

"Perfect." And she was. She planted a lazy kiss upon his ear. "Happy anniversary," she whispered.

An eye stretched open. "Already? Is it past midnight?"

"I think so."

"Hmm." His head rose slightly. "The champagne . . ."

"We left it in the snow to cool," she remembered.

"I think it's probably frozen," he moaned. "I'll go get it."

Ashby pulled him close. "Do you have to?"

He nodded. "Besides, if we don't throw a few logs in the stove, we'll freeze, too." His voice softened. "There's something else I want to get, too."

They stoked the fire, drank the champagne from Donald Duck glasses and hugged each other close. Then Brian produced a small box. "For you," he said, slipping the box onto the palm of her hand.

She pulled at the bow, lifted the lid and removed a layer of cotton, then pulled a thick, gold chain from the box. "Brian, it's beautiful."

He took it from her and slipped the chain over her head. It hung in a V between her breasts. He traced the circle with a finger. "A symbol of unending love," he said.

"I love it and the sentiment most of all." It felt cool against her warm skin.

"I'm glad." He smiled, pleased. "I thought it might look nice with your sapphire pendant."

Her stomach lurched as she stared at the empty chair.

"Babe, are you all right?"

She managed a weak smile and blinked back tears. "It's just that—" she blotted the tears with the palm of her hand "—I have something for you, too."

Silently she handed Brian a large box wrapped in gold and tied with a huge bow. She shut her eyes and rubbed them, trying to dislodge an image: a small girl, wearing a pale lilac evening dress....

He opened the box with agonizing slowness, untying the bow, then undoing the tape, piece by piece. Ashby held her breath as he rummaged through the plastic peanuts and pulled out a sheet of paper. He blinked, then simply stared. "A check. It's for a fortune!"

"Not quite," she said, "but a nice sum."

"Your . . . mother?"

She shook her head. "Aunt Amanda, sort of. . . ."

He looked puzzled. "But you don't have an Aunt Amanda."

"Great-Great-Aunt Amanda." She waved a hand. She'd lost count of how many generations it had been.

His eyes lighted with recognition. "Amanda of the sapphire pendant."

"That's right."

"But you never . . . she's been dead . . . How could she give you the money?" And then his face darkened. "You sold it," he said, still disbelieving. "The priceless pendant."

"Precious, but not priceless. It's worth just about enough to tide us over until the Boston Marathon."

He shook his head, slowly, sadly. "I'm stunned. How . . . ?"

"I had it appraised." She gestured. "Turns out it was valuable."

"Valuable? It was the most precious thing you had."

She shook her head. "You are," she said. "The pendant's only jewelry."

"It was irreplaceable, its value beyond money."

"Yes," she agreed. "Our ticket to the Olympics."

"But it was something we wanted for our daughter."

Ashby bit her lower lip, as if she could bite back second thoughts. She lifted her chin with new resolve. "There are some things more precious to give our children—the importance of doing the best you can. I'd rather be able to tell them about how Aunt Amanda's pendant enabled us to be Olympians."

Brian gave a slow sigh and rubbed his forehead. "Your Aunt Amanda is probably turning over in her grave."

"I don't think so. In fact I think she'd approve. She knew something about taking risks. She came over from England at the turn of the century, betrothed to an unknown suitor. Just before she left home, her mother gave her the pendant. If her fiancé turned out to be coarse and common, she could pawn the pendant and use the money to pay her passage home. It was her ticket to freedom, just like it's ours."

"But you loved that pendant," he argued. "We could have found some other way."

She silenced his protest with a firm kiss. "This is something I want to do for us."

Brian felt a mix of emotions swirl through him: love, awe, regret. He was overwhelmed by the magnitude of her sacrifice. She'd sold her most precious possession. "Are you very sure about this?"

"Absolutely!"

He reached out and took the gold necklace between his fingers. "It looks so empty," he said, a little sadly.

"That's just temporary." She tossed her head defiantly, refusing to feel regret. "I'm hoping to have something else to wear on the chain very soon." Her smile broadened and lighted up her face. "I think an Olympic medal would look perfect on it."

"So do I," he agreed as he stared lovingly into priceless, sapphire eyes.

7

"CUT THE CAKE," Gina urged, placing the surgical scalpel in Ashby's hand.

"How many pieces?" Ashby glanced at the sea of smiling faces crowding the hospital conference room for their goodbye party.

"Dozens," Gina guessed. "Better make the pieces small. We all want a taste of your dream."

The giant cake was artistically decorated with two runners, each with a gold medal around their neck. Ashby dexterously carved the first piece to include the emblem and handed it to Brian. "Your first Olympic medal," she said, grinning, "but not your last."

The crowd cheered as Brian popped a bite into his mouth. "Chocolate, my favorite kind."

"No," Ashby reminded with a grin. "Gold's your favorite."

"To win," Brian agreed, "not to eat."

As Ashby cut the cake she was seized by the recognition that this was finally it. After months of talking about training full-time, they were really doing it. They'd deposited the money from the sale of the pendant in their savings account, worked out a detailed budget, then resigned from their jobs.

It was a moment that they'd been eagerly anticipating, but now that it had finally arrived, Ashby found it unexpectedly bittersweet. She glanced around the hospital conference room that had been the scene of hundreds of staff meetings and dozens of parties, and realized that this would be the last time she'd be here. This place, these people, the routine had been part of her life for the past five years. When she left this afternoon, she would be ending an important chapter.

Tomorrow morning their life would be completely different. Her stomach fluttered. It was so safe, so secure here, surrounded by friends. After today there would be no certainty, no security at all.

Someone handed Ashby a white paper cup filled with champagne. Dr. Gleason, the hospital administrator, importantly raised his hand, signaling for silence.

"We wish you both the best of luck," he said as the group quieted. "We won't forget you. We have a few things so that you won't forget us, either." He grinned and motioned toward two nurses, who wheeled in a large object draped in a sheet. "For Brian," he said. "As an administrator emeritus, we thought we should present you with an endowed chair."

The crowd roared as Dr. Gleason pulled the sheet away, revealing Brian's desk chair. Its back had been set to a reclining position, and plopped in the chair sat a human form, constructed of pillows, bandages and hospital mops. The model was sleeping. "Just so you don't forget staff meetings," Dr. Gleason said, struggling to keep a straight face.

"Thanks!" Brian grinned good-naturedly and pointed toward the chair. "Some of my best work was done like that."

"We noticed," Dr. Gleason said dryly. "And now for Ashby." He paused, his lips curving. "No doubt Ashby's patients will miss her expertise in physical therapy. But as for the staff, we'll miss her magic hands. Most of us have at some time or other wandered back to Ashby's cubbyhole in the physical therapy department for some quick relief for a sore back or shoulders, and Ashby's skilled fingers always found a way to soothe the pain." Dr. Gleason pulled a matched set of stuffed surgical gloves from a pillowcase. "Just to let you know you're handy to have around."

Ashby grimaced at his pun. "In other words—" she laughed as she fingered the rubbery hands "—you're telling me that I'm known around here as a soft touch."

But Ashby discovered that wasn't all she was known for. For the next few hours, as friends drifted in and out, she realized what an integral part of the hospital she and Brian had been. She was touched by the good wishes, both from friends she knew well and from other people she'd merely smiled at in the halls.

Finally it was over. The champagne was gone, the cake reduced to crumbs, and most of the staff had drifted away for another interminable meeting. Ashby stood outside the glass door and watched the familiar gathering, of which she was no longer a part.

Brian placed a hand on her shoulder. "Time to go," he said quietly.

They gathered their belongings and headed through the door marked Exit.

When they reached the parking lot, Ashby turned. As she stared back at the imposing brick facade, she felt a moment of sheer panic, as if her lifeline had been cut.

Sensing her mood, Brian took her hand and held it tight. "Don't worry," he assured her, "it will work out fine."

Ashby smiled. "I know. I'm just a little scared. Somehow, all of a sudden it seems like such a big step."

He grinned. "A leap of faith."

They stood there for several minutes without talking, Brian staring at the third-floor window of his office; Ashby thinking of the patients who had become friends. Around them staff and patients hurried by. An ambulance raced toward the emergency ward; a baby cried. But they did not move.

After some moments she squeezed Brian's hand. "I'm ready," she said.

He smiled and nodded. They turned and walked to their car.

"At last we're on our way," Brian said quietly.

And as they walked hand in hand from the hospital, Ashby knew that they had taken the final, irreversible plunge: she had looked back for the last time.

BRIAN UTTERED A LOW WHISTLE as Ashby came down the stairs. "Where'd that come from?" he asked as he took in the vision of Ashby's slim body wrapped in a hot pink, skintight running suit. His eyes roamed slowly over the slight mound of her breasts, the S of her lower back and buns, and finally the taut muscles of her legs. His lips curled in appreciation. "Is that new?"

"I won it in the Amherst 10-K last spring."

"I never saw it before."

"It's been hiding in my dresser, while I got up the courage to wear it. It feels terrific—no weight at all, but on the other hand," she said, glancing self-consciously at her hips, "it leaves nothing to the imagination."

Brian's gaze strayed to her hips and his smile broadened. "If you only knew what I'm imagining."

"From the look on your face I don't have to imagine." Ashby's cheeks turned a soft pink. "No doubt you're thinking about a hard, fast ten-mile run."

"Very fast and very hard," he drawled, "followed by a very cold shower." He tilted his head slightly. "Are you going to wear this in Sanibel?" Sanibel was the upcoming half-marathon on Florida's Gulf Coast, two weeks away.

"In public?"

"Why not? You look . . . terrific."

"I'd be too worried about whether my stomach stuck out and if my hips were too big. I prefer racing in singlets and shorts and just blending in."

"So why now?"

"Inspired by the weather. Sixty degrees in February! Besides, I thought it was okay between consenting adults."

Brian drew in a sharp breath. "Consenting is hardly the word." He ran a finger along the length of the suit. "And okay is an understatement. I'm practically begging."

She laughed. "You don't look so bad yourself. Legs." She glanced at his thick calves, coated with fuzzy, reddish hair. "Its been months since I've seen legs."

"And probably months till you see them again. The weatherman says today's just a tease. Canadian cold front moving in. We'd better enjoy it while we can."

Ashby stretched slowly, bending in a graceful U, her palms touching the floor. "Exactly what I intend to do."

They stepped onto the porch, and a sultry breeze tugged at her hair, pulling a few strands free of its pins. The strands whipped against her face, and she didn't bother to push them back.

Boston's winter was normally a succession of gray, cold days. So today's blue sky, broken by a few thin, gauzy clouds, was a special treat. Her arms reached overhead in a final stretch. "This makes me feel like playing hooky," she said.

"You can't," Brian reminded her. "Nothing to play hooky from. You're unemployed."

"Just unpaid," she quipped. It had been almost a month since they'd left their jobs, but Ashby thought they'd never worked harder. They ran over one hundred miles a week, normally a run in the morning and another in the afternoon. Once a week they did a long run—fifteen or more miles. They also did track work—timed intervals—to build speed. And in between they sandwiched weight training and swimming. Ashby had introduced Brian to yoga, and now daily sessions of the ancient Oriental art of slow stretches and relaxation had been added to their schedule, as well.

"Let's have fun today," Ashby said, drinking in the warm air. "It's too beautiful to hurry."

Brian nodded. "We did fifteen miles yesterday, so we've earned an easy run. How about the path along the Charles?"

"Sounds perfect."

They jogged side by side at an easy pace. The trees were still bare and brown. Spring was weeks away, but nevertheless Ashby looked for the first signs: a greening bud, the first robin. Sometimes, distracted by the rigors of competition, she forgot about this very best part of running—being outdoors, moving at just the perfect speed to witness the slow unfolding of nature.

Brian brushed his hand playfully against her buns. "How are your legs?"

"Fine, no stiffness at all."

When they'd first begun training intensively, her muscles seemed to ache almost all the time. Now she hardly felt any stiffness, even the day after long, strenuous runs. She was gradually shaving precious seconds off her track workouts, and was whittling away at her ten-mile time. And despite the strenuous schedule she was feeling energetic.

She glanced toward Brian and felt pleased. His face had filled out, and he'd put on a few, needed pounds. Ashby was euphoric about their progress and their prospects. Not for one minute did she regret financing their freedom with Aunt Amanda's pendant.

Her body warm, she increased her gait, her stride graceful and fluid. "I think I could run all day."

"I know. Some days it just seems effortless."

Ashby loved the day after their long run. They had the luxury of running slowly and easily. Most days Brian ran ahead, his pace somewhat faster, but on their easy day they ran together. That allowed them to talk, and solutions to problems that had often eluded them were often found while they ran. It was as if the even rhythms of their bodies swept the cobwebs from their brains.

This afternoon her thoughts drifted to the upcoming race in Florida. "What's the gossip on the Sanibel race?" she asked.

"It seems like every runner of the East Coast is entered." Brian tossed out the names of some world-class runners, who wouldn't normally be expected to enter the local race. "With this cold winter, it seems everyone's looking for an excuse to go south." His jaw tightened. "It'll be a good chance for us to size up our competition." *Size up or be cut down to size*, he thought.

Ashby noticed that his eyes had suddenly become serious. "What are our chances?"

"I think you'll do very well."

Brian's assessment was cautious. It was still too early to predict, and anything could happen. But Ashby had simply zoomed since she'd been training full-time, as if weights had been lifted from her shoulders. He couldn't wait to see her talents put to the test in Florida.

"Well," she said and beamed, "I've got a first-rate coach."

"You've got first-rate talent."

Brian liked to think that her improvement was the result of his coaching. But he'd long ago realized that while a coach could motivate, observe and make suggestions, without talent and—most importantly— motivation, even the best coach in the world wouldn't matter. Still, he was proud of the part he'd played and took no small measure of satisfaction from her improvement. "I think you may surprise some people," he predicted.

"I think *we* may surprise some people," she corrected him.

"I hope." Brian was less optimistic about his own chances. The field of top men was larger, the competition more intense. He'd need to be at his best—and have a large dose of luck—to place well in Florida. A good finish would give him a real boost of confidence. A poor one... He swallowed hard. He didn't even want to think about that.

"Julie Dankers will be there, testing the waters." Julie had won a bronze medal at the last Olympics. Then she'd had a baby and dropped out. She was considering a comeback.

"I hear she's working with Atlee again," Brian said.

Roger Atlee was something of a mythical figure in the world of women's running. A former Olympic medalist, he had turned his talent for coaching and his knack of garnering media attention to the women's marathon. When Atlee had started working with Julie, she'd been an unknown. He was credited with molding and motivating her, transforming her into an Olympic runner.

"They'll be a tough combination." Brian felt his face tighten.

Ashby nodded. She'd heard Roger talk at a runner's clinic and been impressed by his professional approach, his commitment to state-of-the-art technology, and most of all his dedication to the women he worked with. She also knew that Roger didn't like to lose. If he teamed up with Julie again, it meant she'd be serious competition. Ashby tossed off their challenge. "I'd put Brian O'Hara up against Roger Atlee any day."

Brian grinned. "And I'd put you up against Julie."

"Don't bet the bank account just yet."

They turned south toward the river. In the spring and summer the Charles was dotted with sailboats from Community Boat Club and sculls from Harvard. But the false spring had caught the boating crowd off guard, and only a few boats were out. The grassy banks of the river were, however, crowded with office workers—ties loosened, jackets stripped off—enjoying impromptu picnics. A couple strolled arm in arm, their eyes trained on each other as if no one else existed.

Ashby felt a tug of nostalgia as they ran by. "Remember when we used to be like that?"

Brian grabbed her hand and swung it into the air. "We still are. We've just picked up the pace."

The path forked and they took the left turn, away from the river and through a stand of pines. A thick carpet of pine needles cushioned their steps, muffling the slap of their feet. They stopped talking, as if hypnotized by the rhythm. As they ran deeper and deeper into the pine forest, the sounds of the city became as muted as their steps.

Ashby became aware of other sounds, louder, surer—the beat of her heart, her pulse, her breathing; then Brian's breathing, Brian's step, Brian's pulse. Running side by side, stride for stride, she no longer heard two hearts, two pairs of feet, the raspy breath of two runners. They ran in perfect harmony. The sounds, the rhythms, the tempi of their bodies had become one.

A wave of warmth swept through Brian, and he knew it wasn't just the weather. The pungent smell of pine, the mingling of their sweat, the scent of Ashby's hair distracted him. He tried to concentrate on his stride, his pace, his speed, but his thoughts strayed. He glanced at Ashby, her face coated with a faint sheen of sweat. *Their bodies, oiled with sweat, twisting, coaxing, breathless; her heart beating against his chest.* He pulled a bandanna from his pocket and wiped his forehead, hoping to dislodge the unwanted image.

He failed miserably. "I'm gonna run ahead," he called, now conscious of an unwanted swelling. He quickened his pace, pulling in front of Ashby. Maybe he could run it off.

Ashby vented a long sigh as he moved ahead. Thighs, rippling, tightening into thick bundles as he ran. Hmm. Nothing quite as sexy... Her eyes moved down his legs to the hard curves of his calves... Except maybe calves, she thought. No wonder she'd gotten hooked on running. Who could resist chasing after broad shoulders, his sculpted arms, that compact waist, not to mention his tight, curvy...?

Brian pivoted suddenly, disturbing her daydream. She blushed.

"You look like you were caught with your hand..."

"Just thinking about the pleasures of running. Great sport." She smirked. "Nothing like running on the heels of a first-class athlete."

"Heels, my ass!"

"Exactly!"

He slowed. "Okay," he said, pointing forward. "You run in front!"

She pulled ahead and he immediately regretted it. Running in front of her, he had only his imagination to contend with, but behind her there was no need to pretend.

The bodysuit left nothing to the imagination. His eyes traced a line of sweat that pooled at her tailbone, then followed the sway of her tightly curved bottom. He sighed, letting his breath slowly leak out. Why did desire take over at the most unlikely, the most unexpected, the most useless of places?

They stopped for water. Brian pulled a water bottle out of his waist pack. He took a long sip, then splashed it over his face and neck. Damn, he still felt warm all over.

He handed the bottle to Ashby. She drank deeply, arching her neck. Droplets of water pooled on her lips, and Brian had the impulse to lick them away. He moved toward her, inches from her face. But before he acted on his impulse, her tongue licked her moist lips, and the ache in his groin deepened. The springlike weather, the skintight suit. A soft wind twisted her hair, sent it flying into the air, and he remembered what it felt like against his face.

He wound his hand around her waist, resting it at her tailbone, and he pulled her close until he felt the heat from her lips. "Babe," he whispered, "let's make love."

She laughed, tossing her head back. "Here?"

His voice was low, his eyes diabolic. "Let's hurry home."

"Hurry? We're five miles from home."

"We'll pick up the pace and we'll be home before you know it."

"Pick up the pace and I'll go home by ambulance."

He considered. "Hmm, that would be even quicker."

"Brian, this is supposed to be a slow day."

"It will be, I promise, once we get home." His lips nuzzled against her mouth, coaxing, teasing, "Just a little faster."

Ashby ran her wet hands through her damp hair. "Please, I don't think I can."

"You can."

There was something in his eyes, dark and irresistible. She reached up, brushing away the swatch of damp hair that fell over his forehead. It felt electric. She sighed, a sigh of resignation, a sigh of desire. "Why do I let you talk me into these things?"

His grin was silly and grateful. "Frankly, I'm not interested in talk at all."

They were still standing only inches apart. If he didn't move away, if she didn't do something, they'd never... Her throat felt thick, she felt a little dizzy. "I'll try," she managed.

Brian beamed and broke into a fast gait. She followed.

They ran fast, then faster still, their steps eating up the miles, measuring the minutes and seconds until they were home. "Three miles to go," Brian called out.

"I'll never make it."

"You will."

He pulled off his T-shirt, and Ashby felt her legs wobble as she gazed at the broad canvas of his back. The sweat on his pectorals glistened like precious oils. Somehow she kept going.

"We're almost at the one-mile point," he called back. They'd run this stretch so frequently, he'd memorized the distance. He turned, his eyes dancing crazily. "Let's race the final mile."

"Brian, please!" She thought her chest might burst.

He turned. "This is driving me crazy. If we don't get home soon, I'll . . ."

"You'll what?"

"Drag you over there into the bushes and . . ."

"Very tempting, Tarzan."

"The ground is very cold."

She took pity. "Okay. We'll race. Give me a thirty-second lead?"

He nodded impatiently.

"What's the winner get?"

"Ashby," he moaned, "come on. . . ." But a thin smile replaced his impatient frown. "The winner gets to act out his favorite erotic fantasy."

"*His?* Aren't you jumping the gun?"

"Sorry," he corrected himself. "The winner gets his or her favorite fantasy."

"That's better. Steve's ice cream, three scoops, chocolate hot fudge sundae . . . whipped cream."

He nodded again. "Anything you want whipped."

"Nuts and cherries?"

"Ashby, is that what you think of when you hear the word 'erotic'?"

Her eyes glowed with mischief. "I just didn't say exactly how I wanted the sundae served."

He laughed. "Details to be determined later." He pulled out his stopwatch. "Ready?"

"You bet."

"Set . . . go!"

Ashby sprinted forward, her legs moving in double time. With the handicap he'd given her, they would be about even—if she hadn't already run nine, fast miles. She coaxed her legs to top speed, and as she did so, she heard his ragged breathing behind her. His footsteps were getting louder, closer.

She willed herself forward, faster. Her arms, like giant windmills, pushed her faster, still faster.

She could hear him gaining.

Damn. She couldn't possibly run faster; she was running at full throttle. But she hated him to win and get to act out his fantasy. She closed her eyes for just a second. *A large, muscled hand . . . rubbing precious oils into every pore, every crevice, every curve . . . her ab-*

domen, her thighs. It worked. Her fantasy propelled her forward. She was in the lead.

But not for long. He was gaining, getting closer, a few yards behind, then feet, now inches. *He pulled her close, against him, his body silky, hard, waiting.* Miraculously she picked up speed again. She felt her face twist with the effort as she surged forward.

Blue shorts whipped past, and she cursed under her breath. She swore, she grimaced. *Two oiled, muscled palms lifted her into the air, onto strong shoulders.*

She caught up; they were even, running shoulder to shoulder. Then like a bolt of lightning he flew past.

Reality triumphed over fantasy. He was still faster. She'd beat him someday—if it was the last thing she did. She wiped the gritty dust from her face.

He was waiting on the porch steps, stopwatch in his hand, pleasure lighting his eyes, his face creased with a wide grin.

"You don't have to look quite so triumphant," she said testily as she collapsed on the steps, her head bent to her knees.

"But I am. Very pleased. I had to work for that win. Must have been some fantasy," he mused.

She was winded. With great difficulty she coaxed a brow upward. "An unrequited fantasy," she rasped as her hands gripped her chest.

"You ran faster than hell."

"You won."

"But so did you."

"What?"

"You just set a speed record—your fastest mile."

She surged to life, straightening her back, opening her eyes. "How fast?"

"Four seconds off your personal best."

Her arms shot into the air, then around Brian, clinging to his damp body. She threw her head back and laughed. "Slave driver."

"Hmm," he teased. "How did you guess my fantasy?" He kissed her, cupping her bottom lip with his. "Pretty soon I'm gonna have to cheat to win."

He deepened his kiss. She collapsed against him, their bodies, damp and pliant, exhausted and aroused, pressed tightly against each other. Her legs buckled, then collapsed. But she did not fall; Brian held her in his strong, firm grasp. "Mr. O'Hara," she murmured, "you're knocking me off my stride."

"In a minute or two I hope to sweep you off your feet."

"Sweep? So that's your fantasy. Brooms and mops. Kinky," she drawled.

It hurt when she laughed. Exhaustion sparred with desire. But as his lips pressed against her eyelids, trailed down her cheek to the hollow of her throat, desire triumphed.

He lifted her into his arms and took the steps two by two.

"Brian, you're crazy."

"Crazed, not crazy," he whispered as he kicked open the bathroom door.

He put her down, her legs wobbly against the floor.

He twisted the knobs of the shower, and the small bathroom quickly filled with warm steam. She was laughing, breathless. He pulled her against him in the shower, their bodies squishing, squeezing, molded to each other.

She pulled at the top of her running suit.

"No, leave it on."

"It'll weigh a ton wet."

He grinned. "My fantasy, remember. I want to peel it off—" his smile broadened "—like a grape."

She obliged. The shower turned her bodysuit translucent. Her nipples and the dark triangle at her thighs peeped through the diaphanous fabric. Brian tugged at the skintight suit, pulling it past one shoulder, then the other, over the soft swell of her breasts, wrestling one free, then the other. He inched it down, the wet, rubbery fabric squeaking as he tugged and pulled. Each tug, each pull of the Lycra against her skin, was a torturous prelude.

Ashby twisted and wriggled as his fingers and knuckles pressed against her skin, wrenching the slippery garment over her hips, then still lower, down the last, precious curve of her buns, to her legs, her ankles, then finally setting her feet free.

Smiling, Brian tossed the suit onto the wet floor.

Ashby giggled as her hands swept over her damp body. "I feel like a fish in some Jacques Cousteau underwater adventure."

"An alluring mermaid."

Brian poured bath crystals into the tepid water and watched as the surface was transformed into soapy-white bubbles, hundreds, then millions, he thought. He scooped up the thick foam, lathering it over Ashby's arms, her breasts, her abdomen, along the swell of her stomach, the arch of her hips. And the thick bubbles felt like champagne against her skin.

Ashby moaned softly as his sudsy palms slid down her legs, the bubbles pressed and flattening against her calves, the ticklish skin on the underside of her knees, lower and lower along her calves, and then with tortured slowness to her inner thighs.

Ashby pulled Brian toward her. He slipped from her grasp. She tried again, this time managing to hold on to his deliciously soapy buns. Bubbles squished and broke as his chest pressed against her.

He moved his hands to Ashby's derriere. "I don't think I can wait much longer," he rasped.

"Me neither."

He lifted her up, her legs wrapping around him like tentacles. He steadied her gently, then slipped into her soapy depths. He moved against her, his tempo fast and urgent. Ashby wound her arms around his neck and held tight, then shivered, shuddered as his hot liquids coursed through her.

Still entangled, they collapsed, tumbling into the steamy, bubbly water—laughing, splashing loudly, slipping and sliding. Lather lapped at the edges of the tub, fell onto their heads like clumps of snow.

"Is this your fantasy, Jacques Cousteau?" Ashby asked as she thrashed about.

His laugh was deep. "Not quite. Reality proved overpowering."

Ashby draped a leg over his thigh and uttered a long, satisfied sigh. "Maybe next time we can skip the foreplay."

"Skip the foreplay?"

She ran her finger the length of the foamy leg. "Skip the ten-mile run," she urged, giggling as she collapsed against the tub. "Less exhausting." She tossed handfuls of suds at Brian.

Brian lifted a soapy shoulder. "Not much of a challenge." Grinning, he carved their initials into the bubbles on her back.

8

SQUINTING in the bright, Florida sun, Ashby cast an appraising glance at the mob of runners milling around the starting line at the southern end of Sanibel Island, a pencil-thin barrier off Florida's west coast. It was ten minutes before the 8:00 a.m. start, and the mood was unusually upbeat and festive. The sky was the color of a robin's eggs and cloudless. A slight wind was blowing off the Gulf of Mexico, and while the forecast was for temperatures in the eighties, it was now a pleasant sixty-five degrees. Ashby noted that many of the runners had rejected their drab and utilitarian shorts and shirts in favor of riotously colored Hawaiian and tropical shirts and splashy shorts, no doubt the instinctive reaction of sun-starved northeast runners to the Florida sunshine.

Ashby pulled a sun hat out of her pocket, put it on and pushed it far down so that it shaded her eyes. She poured a generous amount of sunscreen into her palm and rubbed it into her very pale skin. She'd feel less benevolent toward the sun after she'd run for a bit, but right now she welcomed its seductive warmth.

"You all ready?" Brian asked.

"I think so." She poured some more sunscreen into her palm and rubbed it into Brian's neck and shoulders. His skin felt taut, his muscles loose. He was always calm and low-key before a race; she was supercharged, like a high-spirited thoroughbred. She rested her hand on his shoulder, as if by doing so she could steady her nerves.

"Now remember," Brian said. "Stay with the lead pack and key in on that group." He pointed toward the starting line, where the top-seeded women—Karen McCormick, Cicily Smothers and Julie Dankers were clustered.

Ashby's attention lingered on Julie Dankers. Like her, Julie was receiving last-minute instructions from her coach, Roger Atlee. Ashby felt a pang of envy. An Olympic bronze medalist four years ago, Julie had already accomplished what Ashby still only dreamed of. Now, after having a baby and taking time off, Julie was considering a comeback.

Ashby's attention shifted to Roger. Even in a crowd of runners Roger Atlee stood out. Among tall, thin runners, Roger somehow seemed the tallest, the thinnest. His billowy, red hair was like a beacon, his eyes were sharp and serious, his face weathered and lined. She strained to hear what they were saying and wondered if Roger's advice was any different from Brian's. Did this world-renowned coach harbor any secrets? As she watched them talk, she couldn't help but wonder what it would be like to be coached by Atlee.

"Don't forget our strategy."

She turned, meeting Brian's eyes. He was staring at the seeded women runners. "Watch for a signal that one of them is trying to break out of the pack. Stay with her and hang in. Now remember, the ice-cream stand is the ten-mile point. It's a likely point for someone to make a break. Got it?"

She nodded.

"Remember you've got the strength to keep up. Take control. Make it your race."

Ashby nodded. She knew their plan by heart.

Brian gave her bottom a playful pat. "Okay, Champ, give 'em a run for their money. I'll see you at the finish."

She squeezed his arm. "Brian," she whispered, "good luck."

He looked ahead, eyeing the group of elite men runners whom he would join, and his face creased in a slight grimace, the only sign of his concern. "Thanks," he mumbled, "I'll need it."

The crowd quieted to an unnatural hush in the seconds before the starting gun. Although she was expecting it, Ashby, wound tight, responded with a jolt when the gun when off. She surged forward.

Out of a corner of her eye she found Brian and gave a small sigh of satisfaction that he was off to a good start, then jockeyed for position between Karen and Cicily. This would be the last time that Ashby could afford to worry about Brian. From this point on, she'd have to devote her full concentration to her own race.

Cicily, running at her side, gave her a welcoming smile. "Glad to see a friend," she breathed. "Lots of new faces, all of them with Olympic ambitions." She grimaced.

Ashby nodded and smiled. She was glad to be running with Cicily. A competitive runner, she was nevertheless supportive of other women. And she was skilled at pacing the race. If she stayed with Cicily, Ashby knew she'd do fine.

By mile three, Ashby was almost forty-five seconds ahead of her pace. That was both good and bad news:

the pace was faster than anticipated. If she kept up with the front runners, she might burn out at the end; if she dropped behind, she might as well concede now. She glanced at Julie in front, and at Karen and Cicily on either side. They gave no sign that they intended to slow. Ashby gritted her teeth and hung in.

Cicily, noting her worried glance, moved closer. "Rumor has it," she rasped, "that Atlee is scouting for fresh talent—in case Julie drops out."

Ashby lifted a brow with mild interest. Whomever Atlee anointed had to be considered a serious contender. Ashby gazed at Julie, her stride sure and steady. "Looks like Roger won't have to worry.... I think she's in."

Cicily nodded. "Too bad. I'd give my right arm to work with Roger."

"Just your right arm?"

"My firstborn, too."

"You think a coach like Roger really makes a difference?"

Cicily shrugged. "Nothing's a guarantee, but Roger's as close as it gets."

The road turned inland away from the Gulf and the breeze died. Ashby felt the full effects of the brutal sun. She could no longer afford to expend energy on small talk, and so they ran silently, neck and neck.

By mile seven, just past the halfway mark, Ashby's thoughts had turned inward. She was no longer aware of Brian or even Cicily by her side. Like a pilot reading fuel gauges, she tried to judge her energy. Half-full or half-empty? Just how should she run the next half?

She ran worried for the next mile, the heated black-top sizzling under her feet. Sweat ran down her forehead, arms and legs and pasted her hair to her face. The sun and the fast pace were taking their toll. She'd slipped back and now was barely dogging the heels of the lead runners. She lost valuable inches, then feet.

At the next water point she gratefully reached for a cup, downing the water as she ran. The heat had siphoned away both her energy and her concentration. She thought about the Gulf and felt a wild impulse to run into the cooling surf, to give up. Sweat pooled in her eyes. Why not? There would be other races....

Frightened, she threw the remaining water at her face, hoping it would jolt her back to her senses and fought against her impulse to quit in the only way she knew: one foot in front of the other.

Give up? How would she explain to Brian that she'd simply dropped out? She closed her eyes for a second, trying to conjure up an image: Brian filling her with a tank of energy. But to her horror, she saw only blackness.

Sweat stung her dry eyes; she blinked, then rubbed them. Her mind filled with another image, wholly unexpected: there was a light with the brightness of a laser, and it was trained on her. The light grew brighter and brighter and as it did so, she got bigger and bigger, stronger and faster. *The source of energy did not come from Brian, but from herself.*

It was as if she'd been pumped full of adrenaline. Her heart beat urgently, her legs moved with new energy. She was gaining inch by inch.

Cicily gave a weary smile as Ashby came alongside once again. Ashby noted there were fewer women— only four—in front. For the next two miles Ashby hung in.

Then fate intervened. Ashby watched in amazement as Julie bent forward, her hand pressed to her side, her face a pasty white. An eerie mood overtook the others. Who would be next?

Ashby didn't linger on Julie's misfortune; she couldn't afford to. Eyes trained straight ahead she passed Julie, not daring to turn around to see if she'd dropped out.

"The gang of four," Cicily rasped, white-lipped, as the front runners trudged along in a tight pack, their feet pounding with the cadence of a somber march, all but oblivious to the men who streamed past them.

And then she saw it, the ice-cream stand, the ten-mile marker. For five hundred yards Ashby ran tentatively, her breathing tight. Would someone make the crucial move out front? The women looked at each other, sizing up the competition. Would anyone take the plunge?

Ashby quickly assessed the situation. The heat had gotten to them all. Their strides were erratic, their breathing was ragged. No one had the strength to risk a faster pace. Her stomach tightened; that meant that most likely they'd run in a tight pack until the finish, leaving the outcome to a final surge. After running almost thirteen miles, the finish would come down to a sprint—a dangerous game of chance.

Their feet pounded ominously. *Brian, help! What now?* The only response she heard was the beat of her heart pumping faster. Maybe *she* should take the lead.

She was tired but not drained. Did she have the strength? Did she have the courage, the determination?

Her decision came in a split second. Still staring straight ahead, she surged forward.

Behind her she heard a collective gasp. Relief? Or astonishment at her folly? It didn't matter. She was out front and she intended to stay there. She could not afford to look back, or to think about the three women she'd just passed.

The sound of footsteps died, except for one set that grew louder and louder. She felt a rush of air and saw Cicily alongside.

"Holy...!" Cicily gasped. "Do you know what you're doing?"

Ashby gritted her teeth. "Winning," she replied, and saw Cicily's face tighten.

"Not without a fight."

Ashby inched ahead, only to be passed by Cicily. For the next two miles they traded the lead back and forth, and curiously Ashby felt energized by Cicily's sharp rivalry.

Then the route veered to the right, and Ashby saw it just ahead: the lighthouse—the finish line. Just five hundred yards. *Just one more surge.*

She pushed forward, pumping her arms like giant windmills. With a shrug she passed Cicily for the last time and exploded like a rocket across the finish line. Suddenly she didn't feel tired at all.

But her moment of triumph was not complete. Instinctively she searched the crowd for Brian, smiling with relief when she spotted him just beyond the finish line. His face was red with the heat, his hair darkened by sweat, but his green eyes were filled with pride, and a smile spread from ear to ear.

Just beyond him, not twenty feet away, stood another man, eyes trained upon her with the intense beam of a laser, and her heated body suddenly shivered with an inexplicable chill. The man whose gaze was fixed so intently was none other than Roger Atlee.

IT WAS HOURS before they made it back to their hotel room, hours filled with an awards ceremony, a luncheon and more interviews and photo sessions than Brian could possibly count. It seemed every sports writer in the East was vacationing in Sanibel under the guise of covering the race, and everyone had requested an interview with Ashby.

"Finally," Brian said as he slammed the door behind them. His hands came to Ashby's waist and he pulled her close, allowing himself the luxury of a deep, unhurried kiss, letting his lips linger on her mouth. "I thought I'd never get to do this—what with all those damn reporters."

Ashby lifted a brow slightly. "Did it bother you? I was kind of enjoying it."

He laughed. "Naturally. You were the center of attention."

Ashby waved her hands. "Fifteen minutes of fame, as Andy Warhol said. I've decided to enjoy every minute of it."

"I think you're into borrowed time," he said stiffly as he thought about the endless interviews. His face hurt from that inane smile. If one more person asked him what he thought of his wife's win, what it was like to coach her, he'd . . .

Ashby smiled as she pirouetted and grabbed Brian around the waist. "I feel terrific."

"Not tired?"

"Who can tell? I'm still flying."

He laughed. "Champ, you were great!"

"Thanks! Brian, I really feel like an Olympic contender, like it's not just a dream. Today it felt like something I could really do."

He nodded. "I'm proud of you."

She basked in the warmth of his praise. "That's even better than winning."

"I feel good about my race, too," Brian said.

"Fifth-place finish. That's very respectable, given the competition." She threw her sandals off and collapsed into a wicker chair, then absentmindedly massaged her feet.

"I sliced a minute off my personal best," Brian said.

"That's wonderful." She flashed a quick smile.

"Ash . . . you know. I really think I have a shot at it, too."

She looked up, her eyes blank. "Shot at what?"

"The Olympics."

"Of course you have."

Brian beamed, but his own smile faded as he watched Ashby's face fall.

"I have an interview at two o'clock," she said. "What do you think I should wear?"

"Anything," he said. "You look nice in anything."

She had gotten up from her chair and was staring into the mirror, a posed smile on her face. "Maybe I'll wear the navy-blue dress. It photographs well."

"Yeah," he said, trying not to make too much of her half-hearted response. Suddenly his own accomplishments felt insignificant. "You know," he said, "I'm within a hair of beating those guys."

Her voice floated from the bathroom. "Of course you are." He heard the rush of water. "Brian, can you hand me my makeup? On the dresser."

"Sure." He was overreacting. He was sure she hadn't meant to slight him. He'd just thought she'd be a little more enthusiastic about his good showing. True, it wasn't a win, but in the long term his record time was more important. It wasn't anything that the press would pick up. But Ashby. . . She should know how much it meant to him.

He watched from a distance as she slipped into her dress. Maybe he was just jealous of her win, of all the attention she was getting. He didn't begrudge her the attention; she'd earned it. She'd won a very tough race. It was just that his accomplishment was noteworthy, too.

Ashby glanced at her watch, then at Brian. "Are you changing?" He was wearing jeans, a casual, knit shirt.

"For what?"

"The interview."

He shook his head. "I'm really beat. I think I'll skip it."

"I think you should come. It's important that we get as much visibility as we can. Our pin money," she said, "will only take us up to the Boston Marathon. After that, we're back to begging."

He nodded. He knew she was right, but at that moment he couldn't quite handle it. *An accessory, like a gym bag.* "I'm gonna collapse on the beach."

"Okay, if you'd rather."

He could hear the disappointment in her voice. Placing a bright smile on his face he continued. "Doing the interview alone is good practice. You'll need it after you get the gold."

Ashby was staring into a mirror, concentrating on drawing a straight, brown line across her eyelids. "Well, so will you."

Brian smiled stiffly. It didn't sound as if she meant it.

The phone gave a piercing ring. Although it was within easy reach, Brian let it ring.

Ashby looked up, caught the exasperated expression on his face, and ran across the room, grabbing the phone. "Hello," she gasped. "Yes, this is she."

She had just applied blush, but Brian saw that her face had gone white. "Oh! Well, that's very kind. Thank you!"

She shot a frantic glance at Brian. "Drinks? Tonight?"

"Who?" he whispered. Ashby's hands were shaking slightly, and Brian realized that this was no ordinary caller.

She hurriedly mouthed something Brian could not make out. He shrugged and nodded. Regardless, drinks were fine, he thought.

"We'd be delighted," Ashby said into the phone. "See you at six-thirty."

She replaced the receiver, and Brian saw that her eyes had gone completely blank.

"Who was it?" he asked again, his stomach suddenly tight.

Ashby put her hands to her heart. It was racing far faster than when she had run her fastest mile. "Th-that," she stammered, her eyes distant, "was Roger Atlee."

ASHBY AND BRIAN arrived at the Sanibel Yacht Club before Roger Atlee, and the hostess courteously escorted them to a quiet table, near the rear of the dining room, which was decorated with a nautical motif. Ashby scanned the list of exotic drinks and quickly settled for a glass of white wine to calm her nerves. Brian ordered a gin and tonic.

Ashby had been busy with interviews for much of the afternoon and so they hadn't talked, although the inevitable question had nagged at her at regular intervals. Was Roger's invitation purely social, the generous gesture of a world-class coach to an up-and-coming runner? Or was the invitation something more?

Rumors about Julie Dankers were floating wildly about: she had opted out of Olympic competition; she was still in, today's mishap just a minor setback. Ashby had compared notes with Cicily and Karen. Neither of them had heard from Atlee.

"What do you think of him?" She could no longer avoid talking about the obvious.

She saw Brian's eyes narrow. "No doubt his record's impressive. But I'm not sure I like his methods."

"What methods?" Ashby asked, her eyebrows raised.

"He's autocratic—insists on complete control— everything from diet to public appearances. And I think he uses his runners to gratify his ego."

"Maybe, but at least he put his talents to good use. After his Olympic win he didn't rest on his laurels and do toothpaste and cereal commercials. He helped other athletes."

"No question. He built a top-notch track program for women in Oregon."

"And you can't knock his success with Julie."

Brian's jaw hardened. "I hear that he and Julie..." He swallowed the rest of his sentence as the waiter brought Roger to their table.

As Ashby peered at Roger Atlee, she thought he loomed larger than life. He was tall and well muscled, his skin very tanned, his red hair untamed, his smile frank, his manner direct. He wore dark sun glasses, but even without them, there was something about him that made you take notice.

"Thanks for joining me," Roger said. He shook hands with Brian, then Ashby, and took the seat between them.

"Our pleasure," Brian said. Without enthusiasm, Ashby thought.

Roger removed his sun glasses, and Ashby noticed his eyes were an intense blue. In fact everything about Roger seemed intense—his gaze, his handshake, his voice.

They made polite small talk for a few minutes, each taking the measure of the other. They ordered a second round of drinks, and Ashby began to relax.

"Nice race," Roger said when they'd exhausted the small talk. Ashby smiled, poised to respond, but then she realized that Roger was looking at Brian.

"It was a tough field and you ran very well. You should be very happy," Roger continued.

"I am." Brian was caught off guard by Roger's praise.

"The men's competition is very tough," Roger said. "I'm glad that I'm not competing now. It was much easier eight years ago, when I was training for the Olympics. Now it's difficult just to get noticed, not to mention winning." He turned toward Ashby and smiled. "That's why I like coaching women. There are fewer really top women runners, and when you discover one, you can really make a difference."

"You certainly have a talent for doing that," Ashby observed.

Roger shrugged. "It's the women who have the talent. I just help them develop to their full potential."

"Like Julie."

Roger nodded. "And you. I won't beat around the bush. I watched you race today and you're good."

"Thanks. I was also very lucky."

Roger shook his head. "Not luck, talent. And savvy. You ran a very nice race."

Ashby thought the room had gotten uncomfortably warm. She tried for a gracious response but her throat was thick, her tongue twisted.

Roger didn't seem to notice. He was looking at her frankly. "Look, I didn't just ask you here to congratulate you." He waved his hands. "I'd like to coach you."

Coach her. He'd said it—what she'd feared, what she'd hoped. Sweat popped out on her forehead. "I'm flattered...also a bit stunned. Coming from you...it's quite a compliment."

"Not really," Roger said bluntly. "After today's race you should realize you're a top contender. And I hope you take it for more than flattery. It's a serious offer."

Ashby glanced at Brian. His face was completely white.

"Brian's my coach," Ashby said in a thin voice. "We're working together."

"I know and I'm sure Brian knows that my offer says nothing about his talent as a runner or a coach. I only coach women—that's why I'm not offering to work with him. As for his coaching, he's obviously done a very credible job . . . so far."

Ashby took a sip of water, trying to collect her thoughts. "We've made a decision to train together." Her decision, her flip of the coin, her insistence that getting there was half the fun. But now, as she explained all this to Roger Atlee, it sounded surprisingly unconvincing.

Roger listened patiently, nodding. "Sometimes there are problems with husbands coaching wives—especially when the husband is also a runner. There are conflicts. Whose career gets priority? And it's awfully hard for one person to be runner, coach, confidant, husband and lover. Sometimes it makes sense to delegate the coaching role."

Ashby looked at Brian, but couldn't read his expression.

"That's not a problem with us," she said quietly.

"You're just at the beginning," Roger warned. "This thing gets very, very tough."

"Even if we weren't determined to do this together," Ashby explained, "I couldn't just pick up and move to the West Coast—" she shrugged helplessly "—leave Brian." She felt her heart twist, as if she'd already done so.

"You won't have to, at least not for a while," Roger countered. "I have a grant to work with some doctors on a sports physiology project. They're at Harvard. So I'll be in Boston for at least the next six months."

"Oh!" She looked at Brian. He was gripping the empty glass and his knuckles were white. "I . . . don't know what to say."

"Don't say anything right now. I know you feel loyalty to each other, and you have to weigh that. But at some point you have to look at this as a pragmatic career decision. Do you want the romantic dream of trying out for the Olympic team, or do you want to make it? I don't mean to be callous, just practical. To get to the Olympics you have to be a hard realist." Roger lowered his voice. "You might have to shed some romantic notions."

Romantic notions; was that what their commitment to each other was? But hadn't it gotten them this far—Brian's impressive time and her win? They were doing just fine. She didn't need Roger Atlee. Her stomach felt oddly queasy. Or did she?

"Here's the bottom line," Roger said bluntly. "Brian's made you a competitive runner. But to get to the Olympics you've got to be world-class." He reached into his wallet for his card and placed it in Ashby's hand. "He's made you very good, but I can make you great." His eyes flashed a challenge. "Think about it, then call me."

ASHBY AND BRIAN stood outside the restaurant. The breeze from the Gulf had picked up, and the strong wind whipped her hair against her face. But Ashby didn't notice. She was oblivious to the wind, oblivious to the sounds of cars and voices.

Roger's final words had stayed with her and his card seemed cemented to her hand as she ran her finger across the raised letters. His challenge echoed in her head. *I can make you great.*

She wasn't sure how they'd gotten outside or how long they'd been standing there. Brian's hand was resting firmly on her shoulder, and she felt the imprint of his damp hand through the thin cotton of her dress. His hand slid down her arm, pulling her close, possessively, protectively.

He pointed to the beach. "Let's walk."

A full moon the color of Cheshire cheese lighted the sky; a million stars twinkled, turning the foamy lip of the waves phosphorescent. They took off their shoes and walked barefoot, arms tightly laced behind their backs, so that their hips brushed as they walked. But despite the physical closeness, their thoughts were private.

Brian tried to separate reason from emotion, but when he thought of Roger's offer—Roger's brash claims—a bitter taste filled his mouth. Of course, Roger could spot Ashby's talent. Anyone watching her this morning could tell that Ashby O'Hara was on the fast track. But it was Brian who'd spotted her raw talent, honed it, helped it mature. He had nurtured it with love. She didn't need a glitzy coach. His love, not Roger's promises, would get her to the Olympics.

He felt his pulse quicken, his logic circle his brain like a boomerang. What if he urged Ashby to turn down Roger's offer? What if he, not Roger, coached her? And what if he failed? He had no surefire guarantees. No fail-safe techniques. No swashbuckling and bravado, no grandiose promises, no gimmicks. Only hard work and love. Was that enough?

A tight squeeze on his hand brought Brian out of his reverie. "I still can't believe it. Roger Atlee offered to coach me." She looked at Brian, her eyes starry. "I keep thinking I could be the next Julie Dankers."

Brian's mouth twisted. "I hope not."

Ashby turned, surprised.

"I hear he was more than her coach."

She lifted a brow. "Lovers?" she asked.

He nodded.

She shrugged. "They were both single at the time. It was probably pretty natural. After all, I'm in love with my coach, too." Her eyes turned serious. "But it would be very different with Roger. He's be *just* my coach."

Brian froze. "So? You've decided?"

"No...." She shook her head slowly, surprised at her words. "I'm just thinking."

"That you'd like to work with him?" Brian felt as though a thousand daggers had pierced his heart.

Her eyes clouded. "I don't know."

Everything that had once seemed so clear, so right, was suddenly blurred and fuzzy. Since the race nothing seemed the same. It had transformed her in a way she couldn't have conceived, couldn't possibly have predicted.

At that do-or-die midpoint when both her energy and motivation had flagged, she'd discovered something about herself that Brian had already known. She had discovered her inner strength, her sheer power. She'd looked to Brian for courage and strength, and instead had found it in herself. That discovery had enabled her to hang in, to gamble, to risk, to win.

Ashby was unable to describe to Brian or even to herself the euphoria she felt. Something inexplicably magical had happened—the ultimate runner's high. Her mind and body had been so perfectly meshed that anything was possible.

This morning she'd transcended the good. She'd glimpsed what it was to be great. And now that craving was insatiable, a raw hunger she'd do anything to satisfy.

A car passed, its headlights catching Brian's face, and in the bright beacon she saw his undisguised pain. Anything? she wondered, frightened by her own ambition. Even hurting Brian?

That one glimpse had told her the cost of accepting Roger's offer. Brian wasn't just her coach, just her husband, best friend or lover. He was all those things, inextricably woven together. If she pulled one thread, would the whole cloth unravel? Was Roger's offer worth jeopardizing what she and Brian had, what they'd worked so hard for? Was it worth risking their future?

Brian was talking, but she hadn't heard what he said. Now he stood still. He shoved his hands into his pocket. "Atlee's got a track record, unlimited funds." He glanced down, then at the sand and the sea; anything to keep himself from finding her eyes. "All we've got is our . . . romantic ideals."

"Is that enough?" she asked desperately.

"It's gotten us this far."

But we still have a long way to go.

Brian wanted to make this easy for her. He wanted to say, *I understand if you decide to accept.* He struggled with the words, but they wouldn't come. He couldn't do it. He didn't want Roger to coach her. He reached up, took her into his arms and kissed her urgently, possessively. He needed to feel her close. When their lips parted, Brian felt an emptiness in his stomach. That sense of loss—that was how it would feel if she went with Roger.

"Brian." Her eyes were pleading. "Tell me. What should I do?"

He stared at the sand, tongue-tied, helpless. "You'll have to decide what's best."

Best for whom? she wondered. For her? For him? For them?

She took a deep breath, filling her lungs with fresh, salt air. She believed in Brian, she believed in them. What had happened to cause her to lose faith?

She pulled the card from her pocket holding it up to the moonlight, so that she could read its words one final time. With one bold, final twist, she tore it in two, then ripped it again and again.

As Brian watched, she flung the tiny pieces into the air. They fluttered and fell like confetti at the water's edge.

Ashby heard his long sigh. His arms came to her waist, and he lifted her high, reaching toward the stars.

"So, Champ," he said, his voice heavy with relief, "looks like it's back to you and me."

She nodded, smiling. "Always has been, always will be."

"You sure?"

Her voice was strong and she smiled. "Yes, I'm sure."

She glanced at her feet, where the pieces of paper had fallen seconds ago. But the tides had wasted no time; the water had quickly lapped up the fragments and carried them out to sea, leaving no traces. *No second thoughts.*

She had made the right decision. She took Brian's hand. Without a glance back they walked away from the water's edge.

9

ASHBY PLACED the refilled bowl of potato chips on the coffee table and sat down on the floor between Gina and Dan, crossing her legs. "Whose turn?" she asked.

"Gina's," said Brian.

Gina took the dice. "I can't remember the last time we got together and played Monopoly." She threw the dice and moved her pawn three spaces, landing on the Chance square. She picked a card and read it aloud, then laughed. "Go to Jail. Now I remember why I haven't played."

"The last time we played," said Dan, "was Cape Cod—two summers ago, when we all rented that beach house. And if I remember correctly, Gina amassed a hotel chain to rival Hilton. Ashby was the railroad magnate."

"Then Dan and Brian got together and made a takeover bid for Gina's chain, offered her utilities, a casino on Boardwalk and a golden parachute," Ashby recalled.

"I don't remember that," Gina said.

Ashby grinned. "Maybe it was Donald Trump, and maybe it was Atlantic City." She threw the dice and landed on North Carolina Avenue. "I'll buy it."

"You can't," said Brian gleefully. "I own it."

She sighed as Brian demanded payment for landing on his property. She handed him the money and counted out her remaining funds. "I'm getting kind of low. I may have to ask the bank for a loan."

"No bank loans," Brian said coolly.

Ashby winked conspiratorially at Gina. "Maybe it's time for a bank takeover," Ashby said.

"Or a chow break," suggested Gina.

"Good idea," said Dan. "Any more pizza?"

"Sure, I'll get it," Ashby volunteered, heading for the kitchen and returning with the leftover pizza. Dan and Gina eagerly reached for a slice.

"Hey," Brian complained. "Are we playing or eating?"

"Eating, of course." Gina laughed.

"I thought we were playing a game," Brian griped.

"That's right," Gina emphasized. "*Playing*. Lighten up, Brian. It's a game."

"Just 'cause it's a game doesn't mean it's not serious," he argued. "After all, what's more competitive than the Olympic Games?"

"An oxymoron if I ever heard of one," Gina agreed. "But this isn't the Olympics. Just an evening with friends, a chance to talk to you and Ashby instead of reading about you."

"Talk about a media superstar. My mother even sent me a clipping from the Fargo, North Dakota, paper," said Dan. "It was that picture of Ashby with the trophy in Sanibel."

"Yeah," Brian said crisply, "the wire services picked it up."

"And I'm waiting in the supermarket checkout line, flipping through *Personality* and sure enough, there's an article about Ashby," Gina said. "Aren't you proud, Brian? Your wife in the national press?"

Brian's face stiffened. "It's great," he said flatly.

"Just media hype," said Ashby, trying to dismiss it. The press attention had gotten to Brian. Especially the piece in *Personality*. Somehow they had gotten wind of Roger Atlee's offer to coach Ashby and had played it up big, with side-by-side profiles of Ashby and Roger. Their pictures had also appeared next to each other under the headline: "The Team to Beat." Brian had been furious. Ashby had written to the editor, explaining that she was being coached by Brian, not Roger. They had printed her correction—as a small item at the back of the magazine. No one, it seemed, had noticed the retraction, and it was now commonly accepted that Roger Atlee was coaching Ashby.

"I'm giving up press interviews," she explained, glancing up. Brian's face was still stiff. "It's too much of a strain. I'm going to go into hiding until the Boston Marathon."

"I know it's become routine for you," Gina said, "but nevertheless, I think it's fun."

Ashby reached for the last slice of pizza and nibbled on it. "Not as much fun as Monopoly," she joked. She waved her hands grandly. "Let the games rebegin."

Brian landed on the Reading Railroad and bought it, then Dan landed on one of his own properties. Gina rolled a nine and remained in Jail.

"Your turn," Brian said to Ashby.

She rolled a seven; it landed her on Pacific. "Two hotels," she groaned, examining the hotel markers on the square. "Who owns it?"

"I do," said Brian.

"How much?"

Brian checked the amount of rent due, announcing the hefty payment with a smug smile.

Ashby counted her money. "I'm two hundred short. Brian, lend me the rest."

He shook his head. "I thought we agreed, no loans."

Ashby looked up, puzzled. "*You* agreed. Besides, I just need it till I pass Go. I'll pay you right back."

"Sorry," Brian said. "You'll have to mortgage your hotel."

"Oh, Brian, you're no fun."

"It's the rules."

Ashby waved a hand. "Since when do we worry about the rules?"

"Why play, if you don't follow the rules?" Brian asked petulantly.

"Okay." Ashby took her hotel off Baltic and mortgaged it from the bank. "Some people only care about winning," she grumbled.

Brian's eyes turned cool. "What's wrong with winning?"

"Nothing. It's just that some things are more important than others."

"You mean it's only important when you win."

"No." Ashby's eyes flashed hotly. "I didn't mean that at all."

"Then what?"

"That winning at Monopoly doesn't matter. It's a friendly game."

"So you can't be friendly and win?"

"Please, you two!" Gina protested. "You'd think we were playing for real properties. Relax, it's only Monopoly."

"Sorry," Brian said, coloring. "I guess I got carried away."

"You have been awfully uptight tonight," Gina commented.

He rubbed his eyes. "Lots on my mind."

"I thought that running was supposed to reduce stress, not cause it," Gina commented.

He smiled weakly, "So did I."

Gina's face softened with concern. "Anything I can do?"

Brian ran his hands through his hair. "Thanks, I don't think so."

"Maybe you just need a good night's sleep." Gina glanced at her watch. "It's late. Why don't we all call it quits?"

"In the middle of the game?" Brian complained.

"Monopoly's never finished," Gina explained. "It just ends when the pizza's gone, you've run out of beer, or there's a good movie on TV."

Brian smiled weakly. "Okay. Let's add up our assets and see who's won."

"Brian," Ashby said wearily. "Does it really matter?"

"Yes."

"I'm mortgaged to the hilt," Ashby said quietly.

"I've go two hundred and a couple of hotels," said Dan.

"I've got utilities and a thousand dollars," said Gina.

Brian surveyed his green and red houses and hotels that were dotting the board. "Five hotels and two houses; three thousand dollars cash."

"You've won," Ashby said.

"Yes, I have."

Brian's triumphant smile sent a shiver down Ashby's spine.

SHE WAS at his heels, running so close that he could feel her heated breath on his neck. They had run the mile on the track hundreds of times, and there were dozens of times when Ashby had almost beaten him. But not quite. In the end he'd always run faster. He'd always won. But this time he couldn't shake her. She stuck to him like bubble gum, fiercely inching her way forward until they were elbow to elbow. Something in her said, *This time.*

But his clenched jaw said, *Not yet.*

Her lips teased. *Try and stop me*, they seemed to say.

But before Brian could bolster his resources, she shot past him like a cannonball. And as he struggled to recoup, she sprinted to the finish.

She turned, grinning, gloating. "I won. I finally beat you!"

Her smile seemed to slice through him like a knife. He tried for a good-natured retort, but his lips felt frozen.

"You did," he said evenly, wondering why he suddenly felt so dejected. Big deal. She'd beaten him in a practice run. Law of averages. It was bound to happen. Once.

Her eyes narrowed. "You didn't throw the race, did you?"

"No."

She tossed her arms around his neck. "So, Mr. O'Hara, how does it feel to be beaten by your wife?"

"It feels..." He tried to be upbeat, to return her good-natured jib, to ignore the dull ache in his stomach, but he couldn't quite.

Ashby saw the strain on his face and pulled away. "I don't believe it! You're upset!"

"No," he said, averting his eyes. "I'm not."

She was unconvinced. "Hey, Brian, remember, it's just a silly practice run. No big deal. I was just having a good day." She tossed it off as unimportant, but her joy had dissipated, leaving stinging disappointment.

"And I'm having a particularly bad day."

"How gracious! You could show a little sportsmanship. How about 'Nice race'?"

He smiled apologetically. "I'm sorry. I'm acting like a jerk. It's just that I can't seem to shake this slump." *Just as you're getting better and better.*

"So it's not your best day. But you're acting like I just aced you out of a gold medal."

He stood stock-still, frozen. That was exactly how it felt. He rubbed his forehead. It was crazy. They weren't competitors. And this was merely a training race. It was just a game they played, racing against each other to spur each other on. So why did he feel as if she'd just waltzed away with the big prize?

"Not the gold medal," he said. "Just the family loving cup. The trophy goes over to Ashby O'Hara's side of the bed." There, that was better. He'd managed to joke about it.

Ashby felt her tension ease a bit, relieved that his mood had lightened. "I'll treasure it always."

"Always?" His eyes lighted with a challenge. "I'm afraid not. You'll have to defend your championship."

"Fine." She bent down and rubbed a cramp from her calf. "Rematch on Wednesday."

"What's wrong with today?"

"What's wrong is that was our final mile. No more today, thank you. Besides—" her lips turned in a smug grin "—I'd like a day or two to savor my win."

"Okay," he conceded. "Two days to gloat, and then I get a chance to regain my honor."

"Your honor? Duels, seconds, that sort of thing? I'll call the cable sports network. This sounds like prime-time stuff."

He laughed. "Schedule conflict. I think they carry ladies' mud wrestling on Wednesdays."

"Their loss. As for us, looks like you'll have to settle our dispute quietly. Just the two of us."

He took her hand and cupped it between his. "I'm sorry," he said softly.

She tossed her head, as if sloughing off the tension. "Let's call it a morning. I'm gonna head for the whirlpool and soak my weary muscles."

"You go ahead. I'm just gonna do one more mile on the track."

He saw her eyes narrow. "You've already done five. You're pushing it."

"You may have won the race, but I'm still the coach."

"It doesn't take a coach to recognize overtraining. Since Sanibel you've upped your road mileage and increased your speed workouts. Anyone can see that's too much, too quickly."

"I think I can do one more track run without courting injury."

Ashby sighed. "Suit yourself, but don't complain when you're too sore to make love."

Brian grinned. "Different set of muscles."

"Well, I'd rather see you use more of those and less of the running muscles." She was being flip, but in truth she was worried. He was exhibiting all the classic signs of burnout—tension, inability to sleep, overtraining. Ashby knew that elite athletes walked a fine line between top conditioning and injury. The trick was to negotiate the tightrope without falling off.

"If the situation were reversed, you'd advise me to ease off."

"I can't. Boston's a short seven weeks away."

"We're doing fine."

"You're doing fine. I'm not. I don't think I'm working to my capacity."

"Capacity! Your circuits are reading overload."

"Ashby, please, let's not blow this out of proportion. I'm just talking about one more mile. That's all."

"Okay," she said, giving in. But she resolved to keep a keen eye on Brian. If he didn't recognize burnout, she sure as hell did. And she wasn't about to let him foolishly jeopardize Boston.

"Go take a shower," he urged. "I'll meet you for lunch."

She shook her head. "I can't meet you. I have that lunch interview. But I'll meet you for the afternoon run."

He frowned. "I thought you'd sworn off the media."

"I have. But this one was scheduled awhile ago. It's absolutely the last."

He nodded, unconvinced. "What's it on today—nuclear war, or Soviet-Chinese relations?"

"I think the topic's modern marriage."

"When did you become an expert on that?"

"I've suddenly become an expert on everything from drug use among athletes to whether running improves sex or sex improves running." She waved her hand. "But at least marriage is something I know something about."

"What do you know?" he prodded good-naturedly.

"That I have a world-class modern marriage."

"Sounds somewhat one-sided. What about the male angle? They should talk to me."

"I'll suggest it," she mused as she picked up her pack and jogged toward the locker room. "Maybe a sidebar."

His smile faded. She hadn't meant to be insensitive; he was sure she wasn't even aware of it. But ever since Florida, he'd felt more and more like Ashby O'Hara's husband—a sidebar.

He turned his face so that she wouldn't see the pain. "Sidebar," he grumbled as he headed for the track. "I've got enough for a cover story."

BRIAN COULD HEAR the irritation in Ashby's voice. "The photographer's delayed. Snow in New York. He's flying into Hartford and driving from there. I won't make it home in time to run this afternoon."

Brian gave a deep sigh. "Again."

"This is absolutely the last time. After this I want nothing to do with the media. I'm even canceling my magazine subscriptions."

He laughed. "It's okay. I don't mind running by myself today."

"Well, I'd rather be running than eating limp lettuce and discussing whether you can be a feminist and married. How did I get myself into this?"

Brian chuckled. "I don't know, but see that you get yourself out of it. How long do you think you'll be?"

"No later than five."

"Good! I should be home before then. I'll start dinner."

"Thanks! Have a good run."

"I will."

It was only after she hung up the phone that an uneasy image flashed in her mind: Brian, running by himself.

BRIAN RAN UP Commonwealth Avenue. In a way he was relieved that Ashby had skipped the run. She hated this route—the roller-coasterlike slopes known collectively as Heartbreak Hill—the nemesis of the Boston Marathon. But the hills really weren't so bad, if you hadn't first run sixteen miles.

There was another reason he was relieved to be alone. He was feeling confused; his thoughts were fuzzy. A solo run always helped him to think, to work things out.

He hated to admit it, but there was more than a little truth in what Atlee had said about managing two careers. And just now Brian felt like an inept juggler, trying to keep two balls in the air at the same time. He was glad that Ashby had turned Atlee down. Just the thought of training without her made him realize how much he depended upon her. He didn't think he could put up with the day-to-day rigors without her support and encouragement.

But he worried. Was he in over his head—a second-rate coach of a first-rate talent? Could he get her to the Olympics?

Then there was his slump. He knew that Ashby thought he was overdoing it, but he was sure that if he pushed just a little harder, he'd break through his slump. And he couldn't afford to do poorly in Boston. It was important psychologically to come out of that race energized for the long haul. And to attract a sponsor he'd have to look Olympic caliber—as good as Ashby. No. Better.

Brian hit the first hill. He took a deep breath, resolving not to let up. He looked straight ahead, his eyes trained on the top. His jaw tightened. He could feel the strain in his calves, but he didn't slow.

It came suddenly—without warning, no pain, no premonition—just a slight, innocent twinge. Then, as he lifted his leg to clear a curb, he felt it—a dull ache. He ran on, ignoring it, sure it would go away.

For a split second his mind considered, then rejected the ultimate horror. *Not that. Not now.*

He blocked the pain from his mind and ran on, uphill.

ASHBY WAS GLAD that this was her last interview. She was having trouble concentrating. Her mind was focusing on just about everything but the questions. She thought about her speed workouts and how to better her time, about what to cook for dinner. She let her eyes roam around the restaurant, gazing at its soothing pink and gray decor. She studied the crystal bud base on the table with its single, pink rose, then the basket of bread. Only then did she turn her attention to the writer, Patti Mac—tall, blond and very serious—a Gloria Steinem look-alike, she thought.

By now Ashby had given so many interviews, been asked the same questions so many times, she didn't have to pay much attention to the questions or her answers. They flowed as if someone had inserted a cassette tape into her head and pushed the Repeat button.

Ashby was explaining how she'd started running . . . Brian . . . On a bet . . . a 10-K. Her eyes strayed to the window. It was a sunny afternoon, and the bare trees were swaying slightly in the wind. Perfect weather for a run. She thought about Brian, midway through his run. And suddenly she felt an odd queasy feeling in her stomach. She looked suspiciously at the chicken salad and pushed it away.

Ashby could tell by the patient smile on Patti's face that she was waiting for a response. Ashby blushed. She'd completely missed the question. "I'm sorry, my mind's wandering. Could you repeat that?"

"I asked whether Brian helps with the housework."

"Oh!" As she tired to summon up an acceptable response, Ashby thought guiltily about dust balls under the sofa, the refrigerator that hadn't been cleaned out since Christmas, and the kitchen floor, which had become a collage of the past month's dinners. "The truth is," she admitted, lacking both the energy and enthusiasm to conjure up a politically correct answer, "neither of us has much interest in housework."

Patti smiled sympathetically, but her face grew serious, indicating that the easy questions were over. "You're training together. How does that affect your marriage? Does it cause stress?"

"Not really." Ashby automatically launched into the reply she'd given time and again. "In fact, it enhances our marriage. If I've had a bad day, I don't have to come home and tell Brian. He knows when something's wrong, because he was there...." Her voice faded. "Just like I know when something's wrong with him." Her eyes instinctively went to the window, and her stomach did a curious flip.

"Brian's also your coach," Patti persisted. "Many runner-coach marriages fail. Why?"

Ashby sat silently, lost in thought. Patti has posed a question she hadn't been asked before, and so she had no rote answer on her mental tape. "When your husband coaches you, you're mixing oil and water," Ashby said after a while. "On the one hand you're asking him to be an objective, often critical observer, and on the other hand you're asking for his unwavering approval."

"Sounds like a precarious balance. How do you work it out?"

"It helps that Brian is also a runner as well as my coach. So he has his own identity."

"What about competition? Are you competitive?"

"Very." Ashby grinned. "We both want to win."

"I guess so. What I mean is—" Patti rested her chin on her fist "—do you compete against each other?"

"No, we don't. Even if we're running in the same race, Brian's competing against the men, and I'm competing against the women."

She saw Patti's brow raise. "You're competitive athletes, and yet when it comes to your relationship there's no competition?"

"Sometimes we use competition as a training technique. In a practice we'll race against each other, but nothing too serious. It's just a way to bring out the best. It's mostly just fun."

Or was it? And if it was just fun, why was Brian so out of sorts this morning about her winning that silly race? Come to think of it, hadn't everything taken on a competitive edge recently? Who did more sit-ups? Who could bench press faster? Who did more track repetitions? She felt her face redden. Even in bed it seemed he was out to win.

Patti nervously cleared her throat. "I guess what I'm asking is really about jealousy. You've been getting a lot of attention lately. How does Brian handle that?"

"He handles it by..." *pushing himself, increasing his training, overtraining.* She felt her body go cold.

There was a strange look on Patti's face. "Are you all right?"

Ashby tried for a reassuring smile, but felt light-headed. She took a sip of water and began again. "What I mean is.... He's great.... My success reflects... upon him."

"So he's not threatened?" Patti asked, clearly unconvinced.

"No."

"Not at all?"

Ashby swallowed hard; the sourness from her stomach had washed into her throat. That queasy feeling. Her hands came to her stomach, but she knew it was not lunch that was making her ill.

With the skill of an expert swordsman, Patti made her final, deadly thrust. "What if one of you makes the team and the other doesn't? If you, for instance, made it, how would Brian cope?"

Ashby felt her mind go completely blank. It was a possibility she hadn't wanted to consider, one she couldn't face. And yet, wasn't that the unasked question, the one that had been dogging them both since Florida? Wasn't that the answer to why Brian had felt so threatened over her silly, insignificant win this morning?

"Would your marriage survive?"

Ashby sat up straight, suddenly filled with raw panic. Not from Patti's question, ominous though it was. She struggled to collect her thoughts. This feeling. She'd had it before. The day her father... She tried to remain calm. But her heart was now pumping so fast, she thought it would burst.

She no longer cared about the interview, appropriate answers, making a good impression, her image. She stood up, her focus moving beyond Patti to an unknown, unseen horror. "Listen, I'm sorry, but I've got to get home, fast." Her body burned with fear as she slowly made her way toward the door.

"Something's wrong," Ashby whispered. "Terribly wrong."

THE HOUSE was empty when Ashby got there. For a second her panic subsided. Maybe this ominous feeling was nothing more than nerves—one interview too many that had finally sent her over the top. She was making too much of it.

Rationally there was no reason to suspect that anything was wrong. Ashby strained to recall their phone conversation. *He'd be home before her; he'd start dinner.* She checked her watch. It was nearly five-thirty. She opened the refrigerator to see whether there were any signs of dinner. Just some containers with week-old leftovers. Maybe he'd run to the store for some food. Maybe he'd taken a longer route or run slower or met a friend. There were dozens of reasons why Brian might not be home, but Ashby found none of them convincing.

She rummaged through her purse for her car keys. Maybe she should go looking for him. But where? Had he said which route he would take? Cambridge? The river? The hills? What if he called when she was gone? What if he was hurt?

Damn. She hated this not knowing, waiting, worrying. She paced an indecisive loop through the house from the phone to the window and back to the phone. Finally she couldn't stand it any longer. She grabbed her jacket and the car keys. She'd go find him. Somewhere.

The phone rang. She jumped, then speared the receiver on the first ring.

"This is Susan Butler at Dr. Nealy's office."

Ashby's stomach knotted with the worst fears: their orthopedist.

Susan's voice was crisply efficient.... An injury...his leg.

"How bad?" Ashby asked, steeling herself.

Susan's voice was coolly evasive. "He's with Dr. Nealy now."

Ashby didn't wait for the rest. "I'll be right over."

BRIAN'S STOMACH knotted as he watched Sam Nealy quietly studying the X-rays. Sam's eyes were narrowed, his mouth thin-lipped. Brian knew that expression. It preceded bad news. He balled his hand into a tight fist, driving his fingernails into his palm.

"No mystery about this," Sam said at last, turning toward Brian, his taut face easing only slightly. "It's your old Achilles tendon." He moved his finger over the X ray, tracing the muscle sheaf that ran from the ankle up the calf.

Brian prepared himself for the worst. "How serious?"

"Well, given your past history, nothing involving the Achilles can be taken lightly."

Brian held his breath. Just as he'd suspected, the old injury had flared up at the worst possible time. He'd first injured it in college, again a few years later. But in the past few years he'd managed to keep injury at bay.

"It probably feels worse than it actually is," said Sam. "Only a tear—you didn't rupture it."

Brian slumped his shoulders in relief. "Thank God!"

"Given your history, you are very lucky. No mystery about the case, either. It's a common overtraining injury."

Sam said it simply, matter-of-factly, but Brian felt the sting of his pronouncement. What he'd meant was, it didn't have to happen. Brian had pushed himself too hard, ignored Ashby's warnings, the signs of his own body.

He'd ignored the throbbing and kept running. He thought he could run through it; then suddenly the excruciating pain had hit. His leg had just caved in. He'd collapsed at the side of the road. Luckily a motorist had stopped and given him a ride to Sam's office.

"I'm planning to run Boston," Brian said quietly.

Sam sighed. "That's in seven weeks."

"I know."

Sam took another look at the X rays. "My best advice is to sit it out."

Brian could feel his stomach twist, then heave. "I thought you said it wasn't too bad."

"Not yet. But any overuse, a sudden jar—whatever, and its ruptured." Sam shrugged his shoulder. "I'm concerned about the long term. If you don't give this adequate time to heal, I can guarantee you, the closest you'll get to the Olympics is your TV."

"Boston's our qualifying race." Brian felt like a prisoner pleading for parole.

Sam uttered a low sigh. "If you're dead set on it, then here's what you have to do. Absolutely no running for at least three weeks. You can work out on your exercise bike and swim. Keep off the leg as much as possible. You know the routine—rest, ice, compression, elevation. And massage." Sam cracked a small smile. "Luckily, Ashby's an expert." Sam scribbled on his prescription pad, tore it off and handed it to Brian. "This is for a mild pain reliever and an anti-inflammatory. We'll take a look again in a few weeks and make a decision on Boston."

ASHBY PROPPED a pillow under Brian's leg and put an ice pack onto his ankle. "You'll be back on your feet in no time," she said, trying to make light of the grim news.

"No time?" He grimaced. "Three weeks—at least."

"It will heal. I've seen this injury dozens of times. The key is rest. It heals nicely if you keep off the leg."

"This makes Boston awfully iffy."

Ashby shrugged. "You can work out in the pool and on the exercise bike, so your aerobic conditioning will be fine. Some runners even benefit from a layoff—come back better than ever."

Brian looked dubious. "It's my own fault. But it doesn't make the bitter pill any easier to swallow."

Not completely your fault, she thought. *I'm to blame, too.* She was tormented by hindsight. If only the photographer hadn't been late; if only she'd declined the interview; if only she'd been running with Brian this afternoon. She never would have let him run the hills—not after their morning track workout. If only she hadn't been so obsessed with her own importance, neglecting Brian.

She sat down beside him on the couch and ran her practiced hands down his leg. *Please, let this be minor; please, let it heal quickly; please, I'll do anything.*

"Don't worry," she said, planting a cheery smile on his face. "I have just the remedy."

"What?" he asked.

Her hands stroked his calf. "Massage," she promised, as she slid her hands up his thigh.

Brian sighed. "Hmm, not bad."

As her hands gently massaged his leg, he closed his eyes, blotting out the injury, his frustration and anger and his fear that his dream was crumbling before him.

10

THE SUN was just coming up from behind the bleachers as Ashby completed the mile. Passing the finish, she jogged slowly, cooling down, allowing her heart rate to drop before running one more very fast mile around the track. The high school track was uncommonly deserted. Normally there were a handful of other runners, some high school kids who hung out around the bleachers, a few construction workers who gathered for coffee. But the morning was uncompromisingly gray, and everyone had stayed away.

She welcomed the solitude. She took a deep breath, filling her lungs with the cold, bracing air, then exhaled slowly, deliberately, as if ridding her body of stress. It seemed as if it were the first time in a week that she'd been able to breathe without that dull ache in her abdomen, the first time she'd been able to slough off the tension that weighed her down like sandbags.

Ashby knew all about what injuries did to runners. She knew that the brains of distance runners produced the hormone epinephrine, giving them a natural high. When deprived of this chemical, runners became edgy and depressed. Like caged tigers, they felt their confinement to be cruel and inhuman, and they expressed their displeasure with ominous growls and deafening roars. All of these symptoms that Brian now exhibited were perfectly normal, and would disappear once he was back to running. But it didn't make the ordeal any easier.

She was totally unprepared for the effect his injury was having on her. Ashby felt caught between a rock and a hard place. Brian had been accompanying her to the track and timing her runs, but these workouts had become tense ordeals. If she had a poor day, she felt Brian's disappointment. It was as if she were running for both of them and when she ran badly, she were letting him down.

But it was no better when she did well. Then Brian's eyes grew uncommonly stormy, his temper short. He became withdrawn and uncommunicative. She knew that at those times he was most aware of his immobility, aware that while he was sitting on the sidelines, marking time, Ashby was moving closer and closer to the Olympics. In the end they agreed it was better if she worked out by herself.

She was finishing now, completing her final lap, and as she rounded the corner and headed for the bleachers, she saw that there was indeed someone there. She looked again, wondering whether Brian had found it impossible to stay away. But it was not Brian.

She slowed to a jog and the identity of the observer in the bleachers became unmistakable: the shock of red hair, the tall, erect frame, the strong, blue eyes.

Ashby turned and scanned the track. There must be someone else; surely he could not be there for her. But there was no one else at the track, and now she saw that he was walking toward her. She tensed with the odd sense of anticipation and dread that only Roger Atlee could induce.

"Morning," he said, as she came within earshot.

"Good morning to you." She tried for a breezy tone, but her throat was dry. "I didn't know you hung around here."

"I don't normally," he said frankly.

"Then what brings you here?"

His gaze was unwavering. "You."

"Me?" She tugged at a strand of hair. Why her? She'd been quite firm about her decision to train with Brian—no ifs, ands or buts.

"Thought I'd see how you were doing," he said, responding to her quizzical frown.

Ashby tried to appear cool, but in truth Roger's very presence seemed to stir the waters. All the same, it was hard not to feel flattered by his interest or curious about his assessment. "So, how am I doing?"

"Stride's good, speed fine." He studied her shoes. "But it looks like your foot strike's a bit off."

"What do you mean?"

"Your right ankle's turning in on impact—just enough to cost you a fraction of a second on each strike. And in the long run it strains the knee."

"You can tell that from just watching me for a few minutes?"

He nodded. "It's second nature."

"What do you suggest?"

"If I were your coach I'd take a look at your shoes. Might need an orthotic in the arch to keep your heel from twisting."

"I'll mention it to Brian," she said, with a sudden tug of regret that Roger wasn't her coach.

Roger pulled a thermos out of his pack. "Got a few minutes?"

She slipped her sweater on and nodded. "Sure," she said, a bit hesitantly.

As they walked toward the bleachers, Ashby wondered why she felt so uncomfortable seeing Roger. Just his presence was disquieting, and talking to him—she felt downright disloyal. She wished that Roger hadn't shown up, and at the same time felt both awed by and drawn to him.

They sat at the bottom of the bleachers, shielded from the wind. Roger filled two plastic mugs with coffee and handed her one. "So," he asked, "how's it going?"

"Fine." She tossed aside the recent difficulties with a shake of her head. She didn't care to confide in Roger or admit that the Olympic path might have a few thorns. "Picking up steam."

"So I hear." He took a sip of coffee. "No secret that I was very disappointed when you turned me down."

She smiled stiffly. "It was a difficult decision."

"No regrets?" His gaze was frank, unflinching.

"No," she whispered, avoiding his eyes.

He nodded. "How's Brian's leg?"

Ashby wasn't surprised that Roger knew about Brian's injury. News in the small runners' community traveled faster than the Olympic torch.

"Better physically than emotionally," she said honestly. "It's tough, with Boston so close."

He nodded sympathetically. "I know. How long is he grounded for?"

"Sam said he'd take another look in a week or so."

Roger took another slow sip. "Look, I respect your decision to work with Brian. But as long as he can't run, why don't you come and work out with us? With Boston so close, you don't want to risk losing your momentum."

"I...I don't know...." Even Roger's suggestion made her feel traitorous.

"I'm working with a small group, just half a dozen women," he explained. "I think you'll find the group stimulating."

"Where do you work out?" she asked tentatively.

"Harvard. 10:00 a.m."

"Well maybe I'll stop by someday...." She was purposely vague. It seemed easier to put him off than to say no outright.

"Give it a try," he said and grinned. "No obligation."

"I guess I could...."

"Great! Come by tomorrow. Early. That'll give me some time to show you around the clinic. You'll be impressed."

"Well, I'm not sure...."

"Nine o'clock," he said decisively as he finished his coffee. He stood quickly, his eyes lighting with smug pleasure. "We'll see what we can do about your ankle."

"Tomorrow? I have—" But before she could continue, Roger had jogged off. He waved as he moved out of sight. And Ashby found to her utter dismay that she was babbling excuses into thin air.

BRIAN WAS on the stationary bike when Ashby arrived home the next afternoon, after working out with Roger's group. Even before she took her coat off, even before she said a word, he could sense her excitement. It was there in the sparkle of her eyes, in her sprightly stride. He felt his stomach tighten into a dull ache.

He gripped the handlebars of the bike as he steeled himself against her enthusiasm. "How was it?"

"Interesting!" Her excitement bubbled forth, despite her intention to be low-key. "A mixed bunch of women, some college students, a few milers switching to the marathon. There's a real group spirit, everyone helping everyone else along. It's kind of contagious."

Like the plague, Brian thought. "And Roger?"

"He's a very good coach. Demanding—a perfectionist. But the women worship him."

Brian thought about Roger's tall, wiry body, his deep blue eyes and handsome face. "I bet," he mumbled as he increased the tension on the bike's gears.

"I can't wait for you to see the lab. They've assembled a team of orthopedists, exercise physiologists and nutritionists. They're collecting training data from elite runners—mileage, diet, physiology, and they're feeding it into a computer. They're trying to isolate those factors that indicate success, and others that predict the onset of injuries—so many miles a week of running, protein deficiency—that type of thing. Then, when they know why injuries occur, they'll know how to prevent them."

"You mean a computer could have predicted my Achilles tendonitis?"

Her eyes darkened. You didn't need a computer for that, she thought. Anyone could see you were stressed out. "Possibly," she hedged. "Roger's also using computers to devise training schedules. He videotaped me running, then the computer analyzed it. Take a look." She handed him the printout.

Brian regarded it dubiously. "What's it mean?"

"It's a biomechanical analysis. It validates Roger's assumption. I am pronating when I strike."

"Then you didn't need a computer to tell you your foot was turning," he said triumphantly.

"But the computer designed a solution—a new shoe. Isn't that amazing!"

"I think it's a little frightening. Why bother running? Just feed your data and your competitor's into a computer, and let the computer run the marathon."

"It's not as bad as all that. Roger says that computers don't replace coaches, they just give them the tools to coach more effectively. Computers can't motivate. That's a human task."

He shrugged. "I still don't like it. I guess I'm old-fashioned. I like to think of running as a contest of human skill and endurance, not a question of who has the best systems analyst."

"What's wrong with using high-tech methods to help you do your best?" she challenged.

"Sorry, I prefer the old ways."

"Like using leeches to treat infection. And cutting off the foot to treat Achilles tendonitis."

"Touché." He smiled contritely. "I guess I'm going overboard."

"It is a little mind-boggling," Ashby agreed. "But I think if you saw the lab, you'd be excited, too. Tomorrow they're taking some blood for a nutritional analysis."

"So—" his feet froze on the bike pedals "—you're going back? I thought this was a onetime thing." Just going to take a look, she'd said. What harm could that do? But he'd suspected it was opening a Pandora's box.

Ashby seemed to be startled by his question. It hadn't been a conscious decision. Somehow Roger had just started talking about tomorrow and the next day. She shrugged offhandedly. "Might as well—until you're running again. I don't like running by myself."

Brian nodded stiffly. He couldn't offer a good argument against working with Roger and his group. Certainly the knot in his stomach—that feeling of impending doom—wasn't reasonable or logical.

She turned and Brian noticed she was studying the computer printouts. As he pedaled the bike, he had an image of Ashby: hard-wired to a computer. At the controls: Roger Atlee. Brian felt a wave of outrage flood him. He pedaled harder, faster. But regardless of how fast he pedaled, how many miles the odometer measured, Brian was keenly aware that he was pedaling furiously in place.

BRIAN LIFTED THE LID of the ceramic casserole dish on the kitchen table and peered inside. The aroma was unfamiliar, unpleasant. "What's this?"

"Dinner."

"But it's green."

"It's supposed to be green."

"Is is Saint Patrick's day?" he asked, glancing at the calendar.

"No, it's green because it's liver Florentine."

"Green liver?" He scrunched up his nose.

"Liver and spinach. The spinach makes it Florentine and also green."

Brian replaced the lid. "My two favorite foods in one dish," he said sourly. "How'd I get so lucky?"

"Well, my nutritional analysis showed I was a little weak in iron and riboflavin. Roger's nutritionist says that's a common deficiency in runners. So she devised a menu high in those nutrients."

Brian looked skeptical. "Couldn't we just take mineral supplements and go back to eating human foods?"

Ashby sighed. "At least taste it before you decide you don't like it."

"Fair enough," he conceded. He bit into it gingerly and struggled to keep from making a face. "It tastes overwhelmingly like riboflavin. On second thought," he said, washing the liver down with a long sip of water, "robbed of flavor might be a better description."

"Try another bite. I think the taste grows on you."

"I think it grows in petri dishes." He pushed his plate away. "What's for dessert?"

"Tofu custard."

His face fell. "Tell me you're kidding."

She shook her head. "Tofu's a concentrated form of protein."

"A concentrated form of torture." He folded his hands across his chest. "I'm calling for a pizza, sausage, green peppers—hold the riboflavins—if you don't mind."

Defiantly Ashby took a large bit of the liver Florentine. "I think it's quite . . ." Her face twisted in a grimace. "Make it a pizza for two," she conceded.

"Look, Ashby, don't you think this is going a little too far?"

"What is?"

"This Roger business. First it's the computer-designed shoes, then the computer-devised time trials. Now the food. For the past two weeks you've been running, eating and sleeping according to Roger Atlee." His eyes lighted with annoyance. "I'm waiting for the printout on our sex lives. Lovers could increase their satisfaction by ingesting Vitamin E prior to foreplay. Missionary position predisposes the runner to unnatural pronation. Orthotic device can increase speed and satisfaction!"

"Brian, really! You're making it sound like *Brave New World*."

"I guess I'm just wondering whatever happened to running for the pure joy of it? That seems to have gotten lost in the high-tech equation."

"It's not lost. I run because I love it," she urged. "I just don't see what's wrong with taking advantage of new technologies to help me do the best I can."

"I think it's a crutch. I don't want to see you seduced by Roger's fast talk and fancy equipment. In the end, winning comes down to training, talent and motivation. Not computer analysis and—" his hands flailed menacingly "—liver Florentine."

"You're too hard on Roger. Regardless of what you think, his techniques are working. I've cut five seconds off my mile and thirty seconds off ten. I think you'll see the improvement on Sunday."

Brian's face had a puzzled frown. "What's happening on Sunday?"

"The Snowball-10-K. Didn't I mention it?"

"No."

"Well," she said cautiously, "we're thinking that it might be a good practice race."

"We?" he asked menacingly.

Ashby swallowed hard. "Roger," she said quietly.

Brian flinched at Roger's name. She didn't even consult him about races anymore. He folded his arms. "Too soon after Florida."

"Roger thinks it's important for me to run as many races as possible, so that strategy becomes second nature."

He shook his head. "Not until after Boston. First make sure you qualify for the trials. You'll have plenty of time to worry about strategy after the Boston Marathon."

Her chin lifted. "Roger thinks I can handle both at once."

"And I don't. As your coach," he said pointedly, "I advise against the Snowball."

"You advice or your edict?"

"My advice!" His eyes sizzled. "You can do what you damn well please. Or does Atlee's computer think for you?"

"I make my own decisions, after seeking the best advice." She sat stiffly straight.

"Fine! Then you'll have to decide who's giving you the best advice." Brian stood, slamming his chair against the table.

"I have!"

"And?"

"Me!"

"What's that mean?"

"It means," she said, struggling to keep her voice even, "that I'm trusting my own instincts." She met his eyes and refused to blink. "I'm racing on Sunday."

"That's final?" he demanded.

"Final," she said, fighting to maintain her composure.

"Fine! Then my decision's final, too."

"What decision?" Her stomach tightened into a double knot.

He stood in the arch of the doorway, his legs planted defiantly, his hands gripping the doorjamb. "My resignation," he fumed. "As of right now, I'm no longer your coach."

IT WAS THE FIRST TIME that Ashby remembered going to bed angry. They had always made a point of making up before they went to bed. But tonight there had been no apology, no bittersweet reconciliation, and she had crawled into bed beside Brian, holding her body rigid, her back stiff and unbending.

They'd spent the evening apart, Ashby in the upstairs sitting room, sifting through professional journals, turning page after incomprehensible page. She could hear Brian downstairs, the television annoyingly loud. Ashby hoped that in time her anger would pass, but instead of dissipating, it simmered like a kettle of water set on a low, constant flame. She felt stretched to the breaking point, caught between Brian and Roger. She valued the guidance of both. If her goal was to do her best, why couldn't she take what each of them had to offer? Why did she have to choose? And why did Brian feel so threatened by Roger?

When they'd first started training, she'd deferred to Brian on technique and schedule. He knew so much more. But now she was gaining confidence in her own abilities, was learning to read her body. She was not siding with Roger over Brian, but making decisions based on her instincts. Running the Snowball would be energizing, not a strain.

She hugged the pillow tight, pretending it was Brian, pretending to sleep. But it wasn't Brian and she couldn't sleep. The cool sheets chilled her body; the rancor chilled her heart. She could hear Brian's ragged breathing, feel him toss and turn. He could not sleep, either. His physical proximity filled her with wanting. She inched her fingers toward him, instinctively seeking truce. She ached to soothe, to stroke, to be cuddled. But she kept her distance, her arms wound around the pillow, her fingers finding them a poor substitute for Brian's heated body.

It would take so little to make up, a hand moving along his back, her lips on his neck. She could whisper, "I'm sorry." She could give up and give in. But those tiny gestures would cost her too much: her self-respect. Ashby pulled her legs up to her chest and wound the comforter still tighter around herself. She blinked away the tears and pretended she didn't care.

"Ashby."

His voice soft and pleading, his hand brushed lightly against her back. "Ash . . ."

She opened her eyes, remembering the argument of last night. She turned slowly, unsurely.

He was standing by the bed, and except for an ace bandage wound around his ankle, he was naked. His shoulders were bent, his eyes a soft green and his still damp hair towel-dried and tousled. She turned from him so that she would not be swayed by his contoured, sculptured body, so that she would not be compromised by the scent of his bracing after-shave, so that she could resist the impulse to reach up and stroke his just shaved cheek.

"Ashby..."

She tried to ignore the anguish in his voice. She ached with a deep, primal pain coming from her very core. She stiffened her spine, brought her legs to her chest and hugged them close, as if she could create a fortress with her body, as if she could steel herself against that ache.

His fingers ran like sparklers down her back. Still she resisted.

"I'm sorry." He said it so simply. No explanations, no expectations.

She turned, which was a mistake; their eyes met. His, so soft, like moss in a streambed, begging forgiveness. She tried to pull her eyes away. But he cradled her chin in his hand and gently lifted it, forcing their eyes to meet. Forcing her to see the love, regret and longing that filled his eyes.

"Ashby, please don't turn away."

With kisses he coaxed her mouth open, teasing the corners of her mouth up, trailing kisses on her eyelids until he persuaded her sad, dark eyes to shine.

"Please forgive me. I acted like a jerk. This injury. It's making me crazy." His lips skimmed her body. Her lips felt like glass, her skin like crystal. And as he touched her, as his hands moved in soft caress, she suddenly felt frail, vulnerable, as if she might break in his hands.

He held her tight, closely as if his body could protect her, could shield them. Could keep her from slipping away. Nothing was worth losing her. His fingers stroked her delicate skin, skimmed along her soft curves. He felt an odd emptiness—what it would be like without her. He couldn't bear it if he couldn't touch her, drink in her scent of wild violets, if he couldn't fold his body around her. "Please, Babe . . . don't be mad."

Slowly her ache was fading, her body warming with want, washing with forgiveness. "Brian, I'm sorry, too. The pressure, it's getting to me." Her face was wet with tears; whose, she wasn't sure. She blotted them with her fingertips and brought them to his mouth. "I didn't mean to make you angry." She wanted to make up, to forgive, to forget. When he touched her, held her, all that seemed important was his love. She crept into the shelter of his arms. "It's all right. All is forgiven."

"I'm sorry about what I said last night about the race. It's so silly to fight about it," he whispered. "Whatever you decide is fine."

"Will you still be my coach?"

He smiled with relief and nodded. "I was hoping you'd ask."

They made up. They made love, their reconciliation fueled with urgency, tinged with the sweetness of forgiveness.

But as Ashby's hands moved along the contours of his body, she was not conscious as she usually was of the strength of his bundled thighs, the power of his forearms, the firmness of his abdomen. Instead, as her fingers ran over his body, she thought about what lay beneath that hard, sure body, about his vulnerable heart and how easily he could be hurt.

Later, as she lay splayed against the sheets, she felt fulfilled, but not quite comforted. With their passions cooled, the ache returned. She twisted and turned, suddenly conscious of the hard edge of his hips, the stab of his elbow, of the ways they didn't quite fit together. And she wondered if there were some things that even their love couldn't make right.

Brian pulled her close, cradled her in his body and held her tight. But despite his strong grasp, his firm resolve, his great, unswerving love, Brian felt the uneasy feeling that she was slipping away.

IT SEEMED IMPOSSIBLE that he could feel like an outsider at a race, but he did. Brian stood on the sidelines as the entrants in the Snowball-10-K completed their last-minute preparations: pulling off warm-ups, pinning numbers to their shirts, stretching, jogging, drinking water, making last-minute trips to the bathroom.

About fifty feet away Ashby went through her routines: retying her shoes, refastening the clips in her hair. Now he watched as she reached under her singlet for the chain around her neck, and could see by her half smile that she had found the #1 charm. For just a second he didn't feel like such an outsider.

He leaned against a car, keeping the weight off his injured leg and observed. She was wearing a silvery running suit. And she sparkled, the sleek, silver fabric catching the sun, her eyes shining with anticipation, her hair shimmering like polished bronze. She looked strong and confident and aggressive. But mostly, Brian thought, she looked like a winner. Anyone could tell that she was a runner to watch.

Today that was his role. He wasn't a runner or a coach. Today he was just an observer.

Ashby had asked if he'd coach her in this race, but he'd thought her request was half-hearted. He's said no, because this race belonged to Roger. Atlee had prepared her for it and planned the strategy; and besides, Brian still wasn't happy about her running it. So, difficult though it was for him to be on the sidelines, he'd deferred to Atlee.

Atlee was talking to her now, giving her last-minute instructions, just as Brian had done dozens of times. The scene was so familiar that Brian had the odd sensation that he was watching himself. Except that it was Roger's head bent toward Ashby, Roger's eyes that brushed over her, Roger's lips that spoke the last-minute instructions. Brian felt a dull ache as he watched and recalled what he always said before a race. He always told her that win or lose, he loved her. Brian felt his heart twist as he imagined what Roger might be whispering.

BEHIND THE MAKESHIFT BARRIER at the finish line of the Brookline High School track, Brian watched the first runners come in. First place for men had been a breathtaking, photo finish, and now the crowd anxiously awaited the sighting of the first woman. He consulted his watch. Any minute now. His gaze drifted to the officials' table, where volunteers were recording times, then beyond it to where Roger Atlee waited, stopwatch in hand. Brian jammed his hands into his pockets. He hated his role as spectator.

The announcer's voice buzzed with electricity. "The first woman has just entered the track."

Brian strained for a glimpse, though she was still too far away. But her identity swept through the crowd, as those in the distance relayed her number—101.

Brian flew to life. Ashby! She was early.

"Our first woman," the announcer confirmed, "is Ashby O'Hara." As Ashby's small, lithe frame came into focus, Brian felt the overwhelming pride he always did when he watched her finish.

Behind him in the crowd he heard a chorus of praise. "She doesn't even look tired."

"Graceful, like a deer."

Brian felt his chest swell. He rushed forward, pressing his hips against the chain link fence that separated him from the track. He waved, his hands high above his head. He felt like shouting, *That's my wife, the woman I love, the next Olympic champion!* But he kept those boasts to himself and instead yelled a jubilant, "Looking great!"

A hundred eyes trailed Ashby as she sprinted around the track. There was something awesome about her sparse, economical stride, her graceful gait. The crowd grew quiet, as if aware that it was witnessing a moment of true beauty.

Then from somewhere behind Brian a voice broke the silence. "One of Roger's women."

Brian swiveled and cast a hot, accusatory stare at the crowd. *Roger's woman.* The words echoed and magnified inside his head. His hands came to his ears, as if he could somehow block them out.

Ashby flashed across the finish line; Brian vaguely noted her record time. But there was nothing fuzzy about what happened next. That image was forever burned into his memory: Ashby's outstretched hand jubilantly holding her first-place trophy high above her head.

And grasping the other handle of the loving cup, his raised arm completing the triumphal arch, was Roger Atlee.

11

ASHBY STOOD in the doorway between the bedroom and den and gave the room a final once-over. "So, what do you think?"

Brian's mouth creased with appreciation as he glanced around the just redone study. Soft, balloon curtains in a soothing, floral print covered the windows. The small desk and reading lamp had been pushed into one corner, and Ashby had moved in a carved oak table that she'd found in a garage sale. She'd cut the legs down and fitted it with a thick pad and soft quilt, transforming it into a massage table. "It looks awfully nice," Brian said.

"That's the idea," Ashby explained. "I think it's important that people be relaxed when I work on them." Since Ashby had left the hospital, a steady stream of friends had found their way onto her massage table at home. "I want the room to look cozy, not clinical—as unlike a hospital as possible."

"Doesn't look like any hospital I've ever seen," he said as his gaze moved about the room, lighted with the shadowy glow of candles. He smiled as he breathed in the smell of scented oils and bayberry candles. "You've turned it into a den of iniquity," he teased.

Ashby put a cassette into the tape deck, and Brian recognized the soft strains of Segovia's classic guitar. She waved a hand and smiled. "Most clients just get the basic massage. The candlelight, the special treatment are for preferred customers."

"Glad I'm a preferred customer," he grinned, as he climbed onto the table and lay facedown, his nude body stretching its full length, his feet lapping over the edges.

"The only preferred customer," she said, curving her lips as she took in his body, still golden with the remnants of a Florida tan, except for his lily-white buns. Ashby felt her clinical judgment leave her as her eyes slid over his tight, compact bottom. "Ready?"

"And eager. Your massages," he admitted, "have been the silver lining behind this injury."

She tossed a flannel sheet loosely over his body. "You didn't have to go to all that trouble. You could have just asked for a massage."

"Now you tell me," he grumbled with a grin.

Ashby folded the sheet back and ran a practiced hand over Brian's injured leg. It had been almost three weeks since his accident and the leg, she thought, was healing nicely. The swelling was down and his flexibility was good. Ashby has used deep tissue massage to help heal his tendon, and she was pleased with the results. But now, as her hands moved up his body, her shoulders tensed. She looked to her hands—her touch—to heal other, deeper wounds.

Ashby poured the scented oil into her palm and rubbed it between her hands. Her body heat would warm the oil and release the sandalwood scent. She loved the way the oil felt on her fingers, the way it smoothed the skin of her fingertips and transformed them into silky brushes.

Ashby rubbed her hands against Brian's shoulders. His skin greedily absorbed the oil. Brian purred softly, and Ashby uttered a small sigh.

Despite their heartfelt apologies and tender love, tension still simmered between them like a slow-healing sore. It had festered since the Snowball. After her win, Brian had stood at the sidelines, his face twisted with an emotion she couldn't recognize. But there'd been nothing puzzling about the coldness in his eyes. It had sent a shiver down her spine.

"Nice race," he's said flatly. And that was all. Brian had then turned his hard gaze on Roger and offered a stiff hand. That was the last time Brian had said anything about the race. The Snowball-10-K had joined the growing list of things they no longer talked about: Ashby's progress, Brian's frustrated immobility, and most especially, Roger Atlee.

And so Ashby, despairing of healing the painful rift with words, now looked to her hands. They could erase the anger, the hurt. With them she could communicate her love. With massage she hoped to heal, to bring them back together.

Her hands worked against the deltoids and rhomboids. She could feel the tension in his arm and shoulders and pressed hard with the palms of her hands, working the angry knots free with her fingers.

Brian moaned softly as her hands ran in long strokes down the length of his spine. His back felt as if he'd slept on a bed of nails, his shoulders felt as though an entire navy had tied them into nautical knots. His head throbbed with a thousand worries and demons: his injury, his recovery, his running, his tiffs with Ashby. He hated it all and couldn't wait till he was back to normal.

He uttered a long sigh as her fingers inched their way up his back vertebra by vertebra, pressing into each nook, cranny and crevice. His sighs deepened into another moan. It felt so . . . good. And as the touch of her oiled hands lightened into soothing strokes, he felt himself relax.

Ashby could feel the stress drain from his body, and as her hands played over the broad expanse of his back, she felt her own anxiety lift, too. She knew that being massaged by someone you loved was one of life's sensual pleasures. But she thought that giving a massage to a lover was an underrated pleasure. It was hard to feel distant from Brian when she stroked his body, luxuriated in its textures: the tough, weathered skin of his forearms, the baby-soft flesh of his lower back, his wiry chest, the velvet fuzz of his neck. She loved exploring every inch, memorizing the shape and feel of every muscle, the arch of his bottom, the rounded slant of his shoulders.

When she massaged, she was an artist, his body her canvas. With her palms she painted broad swaths across his body, her fingers carved bold strokes, and her fingertips etched exquisite detail. Ashby took a long breath, soaking in the scent of the oils now mingled with Brian's masculine scent, the combination oddly intoxicating.

Brian shut his eyes, curling his toes as her fingers pushed deeply against his tight muscles. His head was clearing. He could feel his face ease, a smile twist his lips upward. Ah, the secret pleasures of her hands. He loved the smooth, slippery feel of her fingers on his skin, the warm puffs of her breath at his neck, the slight tease of her hair as it brushed his arms. And as her hands moved down over the sensitive serratus muscles of his chest and side, then lower and lower, he arched his back and moaned quietly.

Her hands were on his legs now, her favorite part— hard, tight and powerful. She loved the way the thickly bundled muscles felt against the slight roughness of his calves.

She took special care with his injured ankle, her fingers carefully locating the trigger points at his heel, the sole of his foot, arch and ankle, applying just the right pressure, then slowly releasing it.

"How's it feel?" she asked with a deep sigh. The therapeutic part of the massage was done.

"Like new. I can throw away the bandages and run."

"Not yet," she cautioned.

"Not until you've massaged every inch," he agreed.

He was at peace, completely in her hands, under her spell, totally trusting. Their tiffs, the tension, the silly arguments had been obliterated. Now he waited, patiently, expectantly, hopefully for what would happen next.

Her touch lightened, her fingers moving in feathery strokes along his legs, brushing, teasing. It felt electric. "Wonderful." The word rolled around in his mouth and spilled out like a soft meow as her hands inched lower and lower to his gluteus maximus, kneading the muscles first gently, then deeply.

A smile ran down his face, and Ashby felt his laughter in her fingers.

"What's so funny?"

"An image. I imagined you as a pastry chef, kneading buns, nothing on except for a huge, white chef's hat."

"Exactly right, except for the hat," she drawled.

He angled his head and sighed disappointedly when he saw she was still wearing her gray warm-ups.

She was at his feet, raking the callused soles with her nails, pulling and twisting his toes. Brian tried to muffle a deep groan and failed.

"You can turn over now."

He obliged with a slow, languid roll, and as her eyes made their way down his body, she could see that his pleasure and desire were recorded not only on his face.

"Over easy," he said, smiling devilishly. He felt like an omelet, viscous liquids, whipped into a frenzy, then quickly heated. He looked into the dark depths of her eyes and felt his heart quiver with love, his body quake with desire.

He reached up, twisting his hands around her waist. "You forgot something."

"What?"

"The lips." He pulled her to him, his mouth wet and moist against hers.

"The best for last," she whispered.

"The best is still to come," he said, kissing her again, this time long and deep.

Her breath became ragged as she breathed in his scent: the dusky oils, the scent of his body, and now the unmistakable scent of desire.

Her lips replaced her fingers, and now they trailed slippery kisses down the length of his body, along the long plane of his chest, his abdomen, his thighs, and finally to his hard, erect shaft, enfolding him and moving up and down in a gentle rhythm. Her lips, her tongue were as sensitive to his needs as her hands, but now her mission was sensual, not soothing.

Brian's hands slid beneath her sweatshirt to her bare breasts. His fingers twisting her darkened nipples. He lifted her shirt over her head, then quickly worked her sweatpants down and off. Brian drew in his breath as he watched the licks of amber candlelight dance over her body.

With strong arms he pulled her atop himself, skin against skin, both smoothed by the lustrous oils. She moved over him, her body trembling with desire, the deep blue of her eyes signalling urgent need.

Ashby guided him so that he filled her, silk against silk. And now she worked her final strokes, deepening, quickening her rhythm until she felt him writhe with a final shudder—the last remnants of his tension pouring into her, then magically disappearing as her own desire welled up and exploded.

They collapsed against each other, their oiled bodies moist, spent, satiated. "You're a sorceress," he whispered, feeling light and free.

He took her hand and held it, awed by its magic. It had stripped him of demons and doubts and filled him with love. He playfully traced the lines of her palm, moving slowly along the one that ancient mystics had named the love line. His mouth twisted with pleasure. That most important line, he noted, was long and deep.

"THIS CALLS FOR a celebration," said Ashby as she crumpled the tension bandage in her hands and threw it into the trash. With Dr. Nealy's approval, Brian had just completed a slow, two-mile run—his first since the injury.

"That's a celebration?" Brian's lips curved with amusement.

"Ancient ritual," she explained, "the discarding of the bandages."

"You sure you should throw it away? You never can tell when we may need it." Brian regarded tension bandages as standard runners' equipment. Inevitably something was pulled or strained.

She slammed the lid on the trash can. "As of this minute I'm outlawing all injuries."

"I'll drink to that!" He opened the refrigerator and pulled out two cans of ginger ale. He handed one to Ashby. They sat companionably at the kitchen table. He raised his can in a toast. "To running again."

Ashby took a cautious sip. "You're sure there was no pain?"

"Not even a twinge."

"Now remember, you've got to take it slow, gradually building up mileage and speed."

He nodded contritely. "I've learned my lesson. I'll be as cautious as a little old lady. If I so much as get a hangnail, I'm off my feet." His face tensed. "I can't afford to jeopardize my chances for Boston."

"You'll do fine. With the biking and swimming you've maintained your aerobic conditioning. So it's just a matter of building distance."

He gritted his teeth. He didn't think it was quite as simple as she made out. While he'd once looked upon Boston as a chance to be noticed, he now had humbler goals. He wouldn't set his sights on winning or even a personal best. With barely a month until Boston, his goal was simply to run well enough to qualify for the trials. And that was by no means a sure thing.

Still, he didn't want to focus on problems just now. Running again had felt wonderful, and now that he was back on his feet he and Ashby would go back to training together. Things would finally get back to normal. The two of them together again. Brian grabbed their training calendar off the kitchen wall. He narrowed his eyes slightly as he counted the days until Boston. "One thing about my recovery," he mused, as he penciled numbers into the boxes on the calendar, "I'll be running slower for a while, so we'll be running at the same pace."

"Not for long, I hope," Ashby said, grinning. "I can't wait to be chasing after your buns again."

"Soon enough, I hope."

Ashby glanced at the calendar. Brian was busily allocating time between track work, swims and runs. She felt her stomach tighten, as she stared at the tightly planned schedule. It included no time for running with Roger's group.

Ashby tugged at a strand of hair. "I'd like to keep running with the women," she said, consciously avoiding any mention of Roger's name.

Brian's face fell.

"I think running with the women is good practice for the Olympic trials. The women's trials are separate from the men's."

"Possibly." He really couldn't argue with that. Despite the fact that it made good sense, a dull ache gripped him. "Once a week should give you that practice," he said, pencilling that in.

"I'd like to run with them more often than that."

He put his pencil down. "I thought we were back to normal."

Ashby bit her lower lip. Back to before, he meant. During the past weeks she'd grown more confident of her own abilities, surer of her goals. She wasn't sure she wanted to go back to the way things had been before, with Brian in complete control.

"We'll be training together," she assured him. "But I think I've really benefited from the group, and from Roger's . . . guidance." She was careful not to use the word "coaching."

Brian shoved his hands into his pockets, his good mood instantly dissipating, his stomach turning over at the mention of Roger's name. He suddenly felt quite unimportant. He stared down at the calendar, feeling miserable, avoiding her eyes.

Ashby hesitated. "There's something else."

"What?" Dread filled his stomach.

She didn't quite know how to bring it up. She wished there was a better way, a better time. But she'd put it off as long as she could, waiting till his leg had healed. "Roger's been negotiating with a shoe manufacturer for a sponsor for the group. It's pretty much a sweetheart deal, no required runs or clinics, no media tours or interviews. Essentially we'd become a team known as Atlee's Feet. We'd have to wear team shirts and the sponsor's shoes to races. But we could run whenever and wherever we like. No strings. And it would provide enough money to keep us going until the trials."

Atlee's Feet. She's one of Atlee's women. An image flashed through Brian's mind: the finish line of the Snowball-10-K. Ashby and Roger holding the trophy triumphantly aloft. Brian rubbed his eyes, trying to blot out that picture, but he felt his temperature rise. "I thought we'd agreed, no sole endorsements."

"This one's different. It doesn't prevent us from training together or running together. And frankly I'd be relieved if we could put money worries behind us once and for all. It's so demoralizing," she said, pausing as she remembered the weeks of begging. "I don't think I can go through that again, and our money from the pendant will be just about out by Boston." She waved her hands. "We've got enough to worry about—your recovery, getting us both to the trials."

Brian was silent. He couldn't dispute what she'd said. It would be a relief not to worry about money. He just didn't like the source. He stiffened his spine. Contrary to what Ashby thought, he didn't think the money was without strings.

"Have you told him yes?"

She shook her head. "I told him we'd talk."

He nodded. "When do you have to let him know?"

"Next week. Boston will be the first race. He needs to know if I'm in or out."

Brian's head throbbed. "Give me a couple of days. I have a few irons in the fire, a few promising possibilities." He refilled his glass with ginger ale, avoiding her surprised look. "I'll need a few days to see if anything's red-hot."

BUT THERE WERE no irons and there was no fire. Brian's promising possibilities were nothing more than a desperate attempt to keep Ashby from becoming one of Atlee's Feet. Just the sound of it set his teeth on edge. He'd do anything to keep Ashby from anchoring herself to Roger.

In the next days Brian worked the phones with religious fervor, calling back everyone he'd talked to in New York, anyone who'd said a kind word, anyone who'd been encouraging at all. He didn't care what the product was or what an endorsement might involve.

The reprieve came from David Seeger, a former business school classmate. "I might have something," he said over the phone, "but I'm not sure if you'd be interested." David was an account executive with a New York advertising agency. "Not exactly an athletic endorsement."

"What is it?" Brian asked, his jaw tightening as he envisioned the worst—deodorants, athlete's foot remedy. Regardless, he resolved to sound upbeat, to say yes.

"We've just signed a new client—a chain of Caribbean resorts. Mostly they've been catering to the senior set, but they want to change their image and attract young professionals. We're designing a new campaign featuring young couples who excel in various fields—banking, law. I was thinking that you two might be perfect for the sports spot."

Brian's heart, suspended, gave a hopeful leap. "What's it involve?" He steeled himself against disappointment.

"A few days of taping in May. Could you get away?"

"Where?"

"Saint Thomas."

Brian laughed. "I think we could manage that."

"Good!" David elaborated on the concept, the schedule and a fee. "Is that acceptable?"

Brian made him repeat the part about the money. It was more than Ashby would earn with Roger.

"They'll pick up your expenses in the Virgins," David assured him.

Money, plus a second honeymoon. Brian rubbed his eyes. He must be dreaming. He dug his nails into the palm of his hand, just to see if there was feeling. There was, so the offer had to be real. "Sounds fine," he said, glad that David couldn't see his grin or hear the joyous beat of his heart.

"Great!" David responded, concluding the call. "We'll be in touch to work out the details."

As Brian hung up the phone, he felt his body collapse with relief. He felt as if he'd been pulled from the jaws of a whale a minute before dinnertime. Money, Saint Thomas, a second honeymoon. He smiled with pure pleasure. Just wait till Ashby heard!

BRIAN WORKED QUICKLY. This was Ashby's afternoon to run with Roger's group. She would be home any minute, and he wanted things to be just right when she returned. He unwrapped the flowers, paper-white day lilies, and found a long, crystal vase that had been a wedding present. He placed the flowers on the plant stand in the living room. She'd see them as soon as she walked in. He chilled the champagne in the refrigerator. But what would make this celebration perfect was contained in the small, white box in his shirt pocket. He opened it and ran his finger along the smooth, blue stone. He'd used some of the money that David would advance him to buy back the sapphire pendant. He smiled and thought about just how he'd present it to her.

Brian found himself humming love songs as he went about his preparations. Suddenly everything seemed bright and sunny. This was the break they'd been waiting for. He felt restored and back in control. Their future would be back in his hands. Now there was no need for Ashby to accept Roger's sponsorship.

Brian beamed as he thought about Saint Thomas. The resort would be the perfect getaway. They'd stay on for a few days, drinking up the sun, enjoying long walks on the beach and making slow, sultry love. His body filled with a warm glow as he thought about it.

Brian stiffened. A noise. Upstairs. The bedroom. His first thought was that he had interrupted a burglar. His eyes did a swift tour of the dining room. A silver tea service was on the coffee table, untouched.

He stood quietly, listening. The noise wasn't the kind that burglars made. He could hear music—Segovia's guitar.

He took the steps two at a time, his fear turning to dread. At the top of the stairs he froze. The music was punctuated by the laughter of a man and a woman. Ashby's laugh—as clear as church bells—was unmistakable. And the man's voice. No mistake about that, either. Instinctively his hands went to his face, covering his eyes, as if he could shield himself, pretend not to see, not to know. But didn't he already know?

The bedroom was empty, the bed untouched. For a second he was relieved. But the relief was fleeting. The sounds came from the adjoining room. The study. The message room. *The room where they'd made love.*

The voice was deep and low. "You're terrific . . . it feels . . . wonderful."

The door to the den was half-ajar, and Brian stood in the doorway, his eyesight blurring, as if he were unwilling to see. But he didn't have to see, he knew: the soft music, the oiled body, Ashby's hands, moving in smooth, sultry strokes.

ASHBY TURNED, her face a palette of surprise. "When did you get home?"

Brian's voice sounded disembodied. "Just now."

"Lumbar strain," she told him. Her hands continued to move across the fleshy canvas.

Brian stared, unable to speak, his eyes tracing her hands as they moved slowly down her patient's back. Despite the fire that spread through him, engulfing, enraging him, his words were eerily calm. "I see."

Brian took a deep breath, hoping it would calm him. But when he inhaled, the scent of sandalwood and Ashby's flowery cologne filled his lungs, fueling the torment.

The body on the table twisted, a head of red hair turned, and Roger Atlee's cool, blue eyes met Brian's stormy stare. Brian felt his rage build. He gripped the doorjamb, not trusting himself, afraid of what he might do if he did not hold tight, if he did not hold on for dear life.

"Rolled out of bed . . . the most excruciating pain . . . Nealy said, 'Call Ashby, she worked miracles with Brian.'"

Roger's jumbled explanation poured out, but Brian no longer heard. He remembered: how her hands, moving against his flesh, had miraculously eased the pain. And then another miracle: how her hands had turned the pain into pleasure. How her hands, sure, strong and sultry had brushed his body with desire. How her fingers had teased and tormented, how the tips of her fingers had burned searing desire into his flesh. *Her magical gift of love.*

Roger's voice drifted through the fog. "It just happened. You know how it is."

Brian nodded grimly. He understood all too well.

Ashby's hands were no longer on Roger. She reached toward Brian, her expression quite odd. "Brian, are you all right?"

He could not respond. Brian simply stood there, dizzy, disoriented, suddenly damp with sweat.

"Brian, maybe you should . . . sit down."

He had to get out. He felt as if he were suffocating, crumbling, dying. And with every ounce of his strength, his self-respect, his courage, he simply fled.

Later, when he was safely outside, when the chilling cold had slapped him into consciousness, he recalled her voice, her footsteps following him down the stairs, and he remembered how he had clumsily knocked over the crystal vase, how it had splintered into a thousand pieces, spilling the delicate day lilies upon the floor.

12

ASHBY STOOD in the hallway surrounded by shards of crystal, the lilies bruised and splashed across the floor. Moments ago the door had slammed with a frightening finality, and now that crash echoed ominously in the pit of her stomach.

Day lilies—each bloom lasted just a day. She and Brian used that flower to mark special days. As she rescued the injured flowers, she wondered, what they had signified.

"Ashby."

She turned. Roger stood at the top of the stairs, his shirt hastily pulled on, his face pleated with concern.

"I'm sorry." His hands turned up helplessly. "I never thought..."

"It's okay. Brian and I have both been on edge." She tried to sound calm, but her hands shook, and she'd broken into a cold sweat, as if she'd just run ten miles.

"Anything I can do?"

She shook her head. "He'll cool down and be back. When he does I'd like to be alone."

She waited. The clock ticked off interminable minutes, then hours. Ashby was certain that once Brian's anger passed, he'd think clearly. He'd realize that he'd misread the situation and come home. But as the day lengthened, as she paced around the house, which had never before felt quite so empty, which had suddenly become cold and unfriendly, she wondered.

It grew dark. Ashby turned on all the lights, trying to counter the feelings of despair that night brought. But instead of consoling her, the intense light seemed to make Brian's absence all the more glaring.

She made frantic calls to the health club, friends, his family, the hospital. No one had heard from Brian. There was no answer at Dan's house, though Ashby repeated the ritual of dialing the number every few minutes and listening again and again to its unanswered ring.

Where could he be? Had she forgotten someone, something? Her mind filled with dark thoughts. He had left in a blind fury. What if he'd gotten into an accident? She would never forgive herself.

At nine o'clock she made dinner. She wasn't hungry. It was just something to do, a symbol of normalcy in a life suddenly askew. She found the champagne chilling in the refrigerator. Flowers, champagne. Her heart ached. She'd give anything to have him walk in the door and share his good news.

She burned the steak, the potatoes were underdone. It didn't matter; they had no taste. She turned the TV to the late-night news. He'd be home before it was over. They'd talk, they'd make love, they'd laugh, they'd forgive. But long after the news, after she'd routinely done the dishes and dialed Dan's number for the thousandth time, she was still waiting.

A HAND touched his shoulder. A blond-haired man looked at him with a curious stare. "I'm sorry, sir. We're closing."

Brian blinked, then glanced around. He was sitting in the dark, in an empty theater. Hours ago he'd gone to the Fine Arts Cinema, where a trilogy of French films was playing. He hadn't the least interest in the films— he couldn't even recall their titles. He'd simply taken refuge there, where amid a hundred people he knew he could be most alone. He had needed a quiet place to sit and think.

Sometime ago, after the film in his head—the freeze-frame video of Ashby and Roger—had replayed for the hundredth time, he had reconsidered. Perhaps they were not lovers; perhaps it was just as it had appeared: Ashby massaging Roger's injured back.

But curiously that realization did not bring relief. Instead Brian's heart grew heavy and the knot in his stomach only tightened. He thought about the past few months, and in the dark theater the truth dawned like a bright light. His injury, his jealousy. . . In the guise of love he had merely put obstacles in Ashby's way. He had jeopardized her chances for the Olympics. And he now knew what he would do. It would be his greatest gift.

"Sir—" the man jiggled the keys in his hand "—I have to lock up."

Brian nodded. He rose from his seat and quietly made his way up the aisle. He didn't look back at the man. He didn't want anyone—even a stranger—to see his pain.

"YOU POOR DEAR." Gina took one look at Ashby's pale face, her red eyes, and threw her arms around her friend.

"I'm sorry to call and barge in on you so late." Gina's face cream and nightgown made it obvious that she was ready for bed. "But I couldn't stand to be there by myself. I had to leave."

"Poor lamb, of course you did. And it's not late at all. I was just getting set to tune in on Johnny Carson. And frankly, I'd much rather be talking to you. Now you just make yourself at home, and I'll pour you a little sip of Southern Comfort and you can tell me all about it."

Ashby collapsed into Gina's overstuffed armchair and gratefully accepted the drink. She sipped it slowly, the bracing taste of the liquor lingering in her mouth. Gina curled up on the couch opposite her. "So, honey," she asked, concern written in her darkened eyes. "What happened?"

"I'm not sure."

Ashby did her best to explain—the simmering tension, the smoldering rift, and the spark that had ignited the explosion: Roger Atlee. She poured it out to Gina, not quite understanding either the pieces or exactly how their dream had gone astray.

"You knew how Brian felt about Roger?" Gina probed.

"I thought it was just professional jealousy. I never dreamed he thought there was anything between us."

"Was there anything for Brian to be jealous of?" Gina asked directly.

Ashby shook her head. "He's a friend. A coach."

"Nothing more?" Her gaze was frank. "Not lovers?"

Ashby gave a grim laugh. "When Roger looks at me, he thinks fat to muscle ratio. As for me—" she shrugged "—there's only Brian. Always has been."

"Even so, it must have been a shock to Brian to find you upstairs, Roger half-nude," Gina mused.

Ashby waved a hand. "It didn't occur to me that Brian would misinterpret it. God knows, I've probably given a massage to half the runners in Boston at some time or other."

"But from Brian's viewpoint, resenting Roger," said Gina, "he wouldn't see it as a friendly gesture."

Ashby shrugged helplessly. "Roger called, said he was in horrible pain. I said, 'come on over.' I didn't give it a second thought. It's what I'd do for any friend."

"Sounds like you were a little blind to Brian's feelings, too."

Ashby nodded contritely. "I thought once he was running again, once he got some recognition, he'd stop resenting Roger. So I ignored it, pretended it wasn't important." She rubbed her eyes. "The only thing that was important was winning—at any cost."

"I don't think you should be so hard on yourself," Gina said quietly. "There's nothing wrong with being competitive. You both wanted to win."

"But I didn't care what it cost...." Her voice trailed off. "Even if it meant hurting Brian."

"You've both been under a lot of stress," Gina consoled her. "What if you gave up this Olympic idea? Would things be okay between you two?"

Give it up, stop competing. Go back to normal. Work at the hospital. Run for fun. Watch the Olympics on TV. And someday tell your children... I almost... I could have... I gave up.

Ashby struggled with these images, then shook her head slowly, sadly. "In the end I'd always wonder.

Could I have done it? Was I good enough?" Her voice was sad. "I'm afraid I'd blame Brian."

Gina sighed. "So I guess you'll have to go for it."

Ashby looked up, her eyes troubled. "Am I crazy?"

"I don't think so. But it's a serious decision. Is this dream worth it? And if you get there—even win a gold medal—what will it mean without Brian?"

Gina's question hit like a hard punch. It left her with an ache so deep that nothing—not all the plaques and ribbons and trophies and medals on earth—could fill it. Ashby felt her heart tear. "I don't think I could live without Brian," she said quietly.

That night, despite the comforts of Gina's guest room, Ashby could not sleep. She tossed and turned, and as she thrashed about, she confronted her worst nightmare: losing Brian.

But it was an even darker, more ominous thought that kept Ashby awake into the blackest hours. If she quit, compromised their dream, could she live with herself?

By morning she was no closer to an answer.

NEXT DAY, as Ashby pulled up the car in front of their house, she breathed a silent prayer. *Please let him be here. Please let it be all right. Just a misunderstanding, a silly fight.*

But when she opened the door, she knew instantly that Brian was not there, that everything was not all right. The house was just as she'd left it: the dinner dishes piled in the sink, the unopened mail on the coffee table, the bruised flowers unceremoniously stuffed into a jug. Everything was the same—almost.

He had left the note where she couldn't miss it—in the center of the dining-room table. With trembling hands she picked it up and read it.

Dear Ashby,
I don't know what to say about yesterday, except that I apologize if I acted rashly. Dan's lent me his cabin in Vermont. It seemed like a good idea to get away for a while and stay out of your way during these crucial weeks before Boston. I don't think I've been doing you much good lately, and I'd never forgive myself if I jeopardized your chances.
                                        With love,
                                        Brian

FROWNING, Elizabeth Clayton spread a dollop of Devon cream atop her raisin scone and took a tiny bite. "Dear, I am so sorry to hear about you two."

Ashby gave a small nod and took a slow sip of Earl Grey tea. Ashby had purposely arranged tea with her mother so that she could tell her about Brian. Rumors were all over town, and it was just a matter of time before they reached her. And as difficult as it was for Ashby to talk about it, she thought that her mother deserved to hear about it from her.

Ashby had another reason, too, something that she couldn't quite express in words. She was seeking, if not understanding, then perhaps comfort. During Ashby's childhood, her mother had made her pain go away. It had been a long time since Elizabeth had been able to do that for her daughter, but feeling frail and vulnerable and terribly alone, Ashby had instinctively looked to her mother for consolation. Now, as she observed

Elizabeth's cool expression, her rigid posture, Ashby felt her heartbeat flatten. She'd been foolish to expect understanding.

"I'm shocked," Elizabeth continued in her well-modulated voice. "You two seemed so happy."

"We were."

"These things happen, even to Claytons," Elizabeth assured her. She reached over and put her small hand on her daughter's, and to Ashby's surprise the intimacy of that small gesture touched her.

"Suzanne, I know how painful this must be. But I feel sure it will be resolved. You must be patient. Give Brian some time."

How much time? Ashby wondered. He'd stormed out two weeks ago, and she hadn't heard a word since. Not a visit or a phone call.

After the initial shock and the sadness, Ashby had felt relief at Brian's absence. Perhaps he was right. Perhaps they needed to be apart. Without the simmering tension she could concentrate on just running. No need to worry about Brian and his running. No need to tiptoe around his feelings. No longer would she feel like the rope in a tug-of-war. But the initial relief had been replaced by a profound sense of loss. It was the way she'd felt when her father had died—the same, aching pain. And then she knew; with Brian gone, a part of herself was missing.

Ashby kept busy with running, track workouts, weight lifting and swimming. She had dinner with the women from Roger's group and went to the movies with Gina. She valued their friendship, but despite her work, her friends, her life felt profoundly empty.

Brian had filled her life. He had given it meaning. He was the one who made the insignificant everyday tasks of life fun. And now she longed to share Belgian waffles with him, to go for a walk on a winter beach, to jog around Jamaica Pond, to poke around an antique shop, to make love in their bed. She longed to just be with Brian, to share his life. She wanted to have children, to grow old with him. To remember and reminisce. And Ashby knew that regardless of how good or great a runner she became, it wasn't enough to make her whole. She needed Brian's love.

"Have you tried to contact him?" Elizabeth asked.

Ashby nodded. "I've written to him," she explained miserably. "But he hasn't answered."

In her letters she'd asked him to write, to call, to come home. She wanted desperately to talk with him, to touch him, to hold him, to feel the warm comfort of his body, to be loved and love him. But her letters had been returned, marked Unclaimed. He hadn't wanted to even read them.

"So is this the end of the Olympics?" Elizabeth asked.

Ashby shook her head. "I'm still going for it."

Elizabeth's brow lifted. "I thought this was more Brian's thing."

"It was at first," Ashby admitted, "until I discovered that it was something I wanted for myself."

Elizabeth's face creased with concern. "Dear, you look as if you've been overdoing it. You're so thin." Elizabeth studied her daughter's plate of untouched sandwiches. "Are you eating? And your eyes look tired. Have you gotten a good night's sleep?"

Ashby nodded, and as if to prove it, she nibbled unenthusiastically on a cucumber sandwich. She'd been following her nutritionist's food plan, routinely eating whatever was needed to fuel her body. As for sleep, she hadn't managed to sleep through the night since Brian had left. She couldn't stand to sleep in their bed. It seemed vast and unfriendly without him, and Brian's scent seemed to linger in the sheets no matter how many times she washed them. Their bed, his scent—it all filled her with a desperate longing.

"Suzanne, I know this is an unpleasant subject, but how are you supporting yourself? You're not working, and with Brian gone . . ."

"Savings," Ashby said, not elaborating.

"And when that runs out?"

"My coach, Roger—" it felt odd using that word "—he's arranging an advertising sponsorship. It should tide me over."

Elizabeth's face tightened. "I'm not happy seeing my daughter selling herself for money. It's a bit common. I don't think your father would approve." She sipped her tea quietly. "Your father set up a trust fund for you. It's tied to the birth of your first child. But I'm the trustee. I could talk to our lawyers at Wagsal and Sher. I don't think it would be all that impossible to let you have some of the money now—" her palms opened like a blossom "—if that would help."

Ashby stared, incredulous. "You'd give me the money?"

"Yes, of course."

"I didn't think . . ."

"You didn't ask."

Ashby thought about that awful dinner and how she'd tried to ask. "I thought you didn't approve."

"Approve?" Elizabeth tilted her head. "It may not be what I'd choose for you, but you're clearly committed. I'd like to help. I never understood how much it meant to you. You don't talk about it."

Ashby gave a deep sigh. "I know." She hesitated to say more. But looking into her mother's concerned eyes, she realized the cost of things left unsaid. She clasped her hands to her stomach and continued. "After the Lexington race," she said, "I couldn't talk about it." Ashby's voice was barely a whisper. "I was so hurt."

"Hurt? But dear, why?"

"That you'd left. You weren't there to see me win."

Elizabeth's eyes darkened. "Suzanne, I'm sorry. I never knew that it would matter. But you see, I didn't leave because I didn't care."

Ashby could barely ask. "Then why?"

She met her daughter's sapphire eyes. "Maybe when you're a mother you'll understand. It's the hardest thing in the world to see your child in pain. I stood there on that hill, watching you climb it—your face creased, your shoulders slumped, the sweat on your face—and I felt so helpless."

Elizabeth seemed to be looking into the distance, into the past. "I can remember when you were born. That was way before fathers had anything to do with childbirth. It was a very difficult delivery. But my mother was there. Later she told me that watching me go through labor was the hardest thing she'd ever done. That's how I felt when I watched you run. But I'm afraid I wasn't as strong as my mother. I had to leave." Elizabeth's eyes were soft, pleading. "I'm so sorry, dear. Can you forgive me?"

Ashby felt her own eyes cloud. For the moment the overwhelming ache that had filled her since Brian left was gone. "Yes," she said as she reached for her mother's hand. "I forgive you."

ROGER CALLED OUT TIMES as the women did speed workouts on the track, and Ashby's face instantly registered disappointment when she heard her time. She finished her cool-down, then waited under a tree some distance from the track, while the other women completed their track work.

She was worse than stalled, she was in a slump. It wasn't just a matter of not improving, she was actually slipping behind. At first Roger had tossed it off as natural, as a temporary slowdown. But in the past crucial week, as she remained firmly in the doldrums, she could sense his concern.

The last woman completed her run, and Roger signaled for them to join him on the bleachers. "Good work, ladies," he said. "Five days till Boston. You're as ready as you'll ever be. We'll shorten our distances and ease up on speed, so you'll be primed. The key now is rest. Don't overtrain, and most importantly, relax. Tomorrow we'll do a nice, easy run around Jamaica Pond." He raised his arm, signaling the end of the meeting.

The group jogged toward the locker room, but Ashby lagged behind. She didn't feel very social today.

"Ashby! Wait up!"

She turned and saw Roger waving. He jogged over. "You in a hurry?"

"Not really." She wasn't in much of a rush to go home. It was getting harder and harder to be there alone.

"Like some coffee?"

"Sure," she said without enthusiasm.

"How about the Muffin Man?"

The Muffin Man. She'd always gone there with Brian. She gave a stiff nod.

Stella greeted them with a broad smile. "Nice to see ya'. How's Brian?"

Ashby smiled weakly. "Fine," she said, carefully avoiding Stella's eyes. She must be the only one in town who didn't know about Brian, Ashby thought.

"Your usual?" Stella asked, seating them.

Roger gave Ashby a careful look. "Stuff in a few extra muffins for her," he ordered.

Over coffee they discussed the weather. "Long-range forecast is for clear and sunny for the marathon. Year before it rained." Ashby was babbling. Really she had no idea if it had or hadn't rained. She was thinking about how many times she'd been here with Brian, that first time when they'd just met, the day after her first race, the morning after their triumphant return from Washington. And now she looked across the table, somehow expecting to see Brian's wide grin, his carved cheeks, his thick, chestnut hair, his soft, green eyes. Her face fell as her eyes met Roger's steely-blue eyes instead.

Where was Brian, what was he doing, was he all right? Was he angry, did he miss her, did he love her? Damn him, why didn't he call? Why didn't he answer her letters? Why didn't he come home? Didn't he know

*that she missed him, that she loved him, that she needed
him desperately?* A physical ache spread through her.

Roger was no longer talking; he was quietly staring
at her, his eyes lighted with concern. "You been okay?"

She nodded and tried to smile.

He raised a brow and fidgeted nervously with his
coffee spoon. "Look," he said, "there's no use pretending. I'm worried."

Her hands were damp, and she rubbed them against
her fleece pants. "Me too," she confessed.

Worried was an understatement. She was in a white
panic. What had seemed to be merely a formality—
qualifying for the Olympic trials by running Boston in
under two hours and fifty minutes—was now touch
and go. "I don't know what's the matter," she said desperately. "I'm working as hard as I've ever worked, but
I can't seem to build any momentum. I'm seeing
Gina—" she waved a hand "—maybe it's a bug, maybe
antibiotics . . ."

"Uh-huh."

"Maybe it's the shoes. Maybe we should take another look at the videos."

"I'll check it out, but I don't think it's the shoes."

"My appetite's a little off. Maybe some supplements. Protein drinks." She pushed her coffee cup away.
"Maybe it's my . . . riboflavins," she said despondently.

"Riboflavins?" His eyes widened incredulously.

"I don't know." Her head was bent, her voice barely
a whisper. "Maybe I peaked too soon, or it was just a
fluke—just a flash in the pan. Maybe I'm just not that
good, not Olympic class."

Roger took a big bite out of a muffin and chewed
slowly. "I don't think so. I think you're very good."

"You do?"

"Yes."

"Then what?"

He motioned to Stella to refill their mugs. "One thing about running. You can be in top form, but emotionally, if things are off it shows."

"Emotionally I'm fine."

A brow lifted once more.

"I'll admit the split with Brian's been difficult. But I'm coping." Suddenly her head throbbed. She placed her fingers on her temples and rubbed. "I can still do this."

"Look, this is hard." Roger was cracking his knuckles, something he did when he had bad news. "I think you should consider skipping Boston."

She felt as if the wind had been knocked out of her. "Skip the marathon?"

"It would be a mistake to run a bad race—bad for your career and worse for your confidence."

She tried to catch her breath. "You don't think I can do it."

"Normally you could do it with your eyes closed, but not now."

Her arms flailed wildly. "It's my qualifying race." Ashby was gripped by panic. When Brian left, her salvation had been running—her Olympic dream. Now that, too, was fading, falling apart. Not run Boston? Without running, without Brian, there was nothing.

He shrugged. "There are other races. Look, only you can make the decision, but sometimes I can see something that an athlete's too close to see. It's not your training or your diet or your shoes. Face it. Something's missing."

"What?" she asked desperately as her stomach turned queasy.

Roger pressed his hand against his knuckles; it gave a particularly loud crack. "What's missing," he said quietly, "is Brian."

13

BRIAN SCOOPED the pasta onto his plate and poured the sauce with tomatoes, olives, peas and carrot and meatballs onto it. Ashby and he always ate this dish the night before a marathon and had named it Pasta Premarathon. Ashby had created it the night before her first marathon, based solely on what she'd found in the pantry and refrigerator. She'd done well in that race, and so fixing the recipe had become a ritual. Even though he was alone, Brian clung rigidly to it, fearing that to deviate would jinx his chances in tomorrow's Boston Marathon.

Brian knew the recipe by heart. He'd made it exactly as he remembered it, not bothering to halve the ingredients. So the rest—Ashby's half—sat in the pot on the stove, a visible reminder of her absence.

Brian was staying in Dan's empty apartment while Dan was in London. The strangeness, the quiet, rankled. Brian tuned the radio to a hard-rock station and turned it loud. He'd had enough of silence and quiet to last a lifetime. He twisted the spaghetti absentmindedly onto his fork and ate quickly. The taste, the smells, the very ceremony of eating this meal were poignant reminders of the way things used to be.

The prerace dinner marked the countdown to the marathon. After weeks of training and planning, nerves were wound tight. But there was also a feeling of exhilaration in the air. Each marathon was a unique challenge, never quite the same as the last one. The weather, the competition, the route, the uncertainties of mind and body always made the outcome questionable, the challenge different each time. And Brian found a special joy in sharing the highs and lows, apprehension and exhilaration with Ashby.

Tonight there was none of that. Instead his senses felt deadened, numb, as if he were only half-alive—like the dinner that was half-eaten and the bed that was half-empty.

The emptiness had taunted him as he ran through Vermont's winding hills. He'd hoped it would dissipate once he was back in Boston. But being back in familiar surroundings, coming home and yet not being home, only made it worse.

Brian knew at once that it had been a mistake to go to Dan's cabin. How had he imagined he could be free of Ashby in a place where they'd celebrated their marriage and marked its anniversary? Her scent seemed to linger in the air; her laughter echoed from the walls. He couldn't stay there; her presence was pervasive, the memory painful.

After two days he'd rented a guest house from a farmer. It was stark and sterile, but there was no memory of Ashby there. And in this banal setting he'd found release from his overwhelming pain.

Running had become his salvation. His leg had healed, and his body grew strong as he ran miles over country roads. But sometimes when he was running, the smell of the birches and pines would remind him of her cologne. Or he would hear her laughter; but when he turned, expecting to see her graceful body running behind, there would be no one. Her laughter had been nothing more than the mocking song of a bird or the wind whistling through bare trees.

It had been a struggle not to go home. Several times he'd phoned, only to hang up before she answered. Once in the middle of the night he had even driven home, parking the car outside their house as he waited for dawn. But in the light of morning he'd realized it was a mistake. He couldn't intrude, throw her life into turmoil at this crucial point. So he'd gone back to Vermont.

As ALWAYS on the night before the Boston Marathon, Eliot's Lounge was packed to the gills. A runners' hangout, Eliot's was as legendary as the marathon itself and, Brian thought, as he shoved and snaked through jammed bodies, almost as difficult to get into.

He greeted friends as he made his way. Although loneliness had driven him from Dan's apartment, he did not feel much like talking. He dreaded the inevitable questions, for which he had no answers. So he smiled, exchanged quick greetings and made his way to the bar, claiming a scarce seat.

"Can I buy you a drink?"

Brian turned. The man next to him raised a scotch glass in greeting. To his dismay, Brian realized he'd just seated himself next to Ted McDowell. Brian managed a stiff smile. Ted McDowell was the last person he felt like seeing just now. Brian recalled the reporter's diatribe about the effects of competition on marriage, so many months ago. He managed a tight-lipped smile. "Thanks. I'll have a Narragansett beer."

McDowell nodded. "And another scotch," he told the bartender.

"You covering the race?"

"My fifteenth. Each time it gets a little harder to find something interesting to write about." He waved his scotch glass. "This place is good for scrounging up local gossip—what my editor rarefies as human interest."

"I'm no help there," Brian said, taking a long swig of beer. "I've been in Vermont."

"I've heard," said McDowell, lifting a brow significantly.

"That," said Brian, "is not for publication."

McDowell gave an imperceptible nod.

They drank in stony silence. Around them runners were greeting old friends, swapping stories, trading remedies and recipes. Several times Brian's spine tingled when he heard a woman's voice. Ashby's voice? But when he turned, his heart pumping with joy and fear, it was someone else.

"You married?" Brian asked McDowell.

"A long time ago." McDowell's eyes seemed to lose focus, and for a minute Brian thought it was the scotch, then he realized that McDowell had just drifted back in time.

"A reporter?"

McDowell nodded. "A rival reporter. We kept tripping over each other. We always seemed to cover the same story. We had a kind of friendly competition going. One thing led to another and we fell in love. Ellie was different from any woman I knew. Damn good at what she did. I admired the hell out of her." Mc-

Dowell's lips curved in an appreciative smile. "She was the best."

Brian sipped his beer. "What happened?"

"We got married, and for a while it was kind of a high, competing against each other. It spurred us on to do the best we could. We were in Chicago, both covering a police drug scandal. Ellie was relentless, had some source inside the police department feeding her stuff. I was getting scooped every day. Boy, was I burned! Couldn't handle it, picking up the paper every day, reading her story, while I busted my chops getting nowhere. Pretty soon my colleagues were getting on me. I laughed it off, but it was damn painful, getting scooped by your own wife."

Brian gave a knowing nod.

"One day," McDowell said, "her source called the house. She was out. I persuaded him to give me the information. I didn't give her the message. Instead I used it to bust the story wide open. She never said a word, but the night my story ran, I came home and the house was empty. She'd moved out. Not even a note."

Brian found himself hoping for a happy ending. "Did you get back together?"

McDowell frowned and shook his head sadly. "I got the Pulitzer for the story. It's a journalist's gold medal—what you work your whole career for. The paper had a big bash. It was the worst night of my life. I drank myself into a stupor. I couldn't face what I'd done." McDowell's voice was a slurred whisper. "The money, the prize—let me tell you, it wasn't worth it. To this day I'd gladly trade in the prize for Ellie—even for a night, for just a chance to say, 'I'm sorry.'"

Brian finished his beer. He ordered another one and drank it quickly. McDowell's story sounded like one of Aesop's fables, complete with moral. But he wasn't McDowell, Ellie wasn't Ashby, and it wasn't his story. And the moral . . .

"Atlee was in here awhile ago," McDowell said.

Brian stiffened. "Alone?"

"No, with a woman." McDowell's fingers formed two circles, like intersecting Olympic rings. "A hot item, I gather."

Brian could barely ask. "Ashby?"

He shook his head. "Carrie Randolph."

Brian collapsed with relief. "Have you seen Ashby?"

"No, but from the scuttlebutt I gather Atlee's worried."

Brian's stomach twisted. "An injury?"

"Nothing physical," said McDowell. He tapped his head. "It's her mental state Atlee's worried about."

THE HOUSE WAS DARK except for an upstairs window, the bedroom. Brian stood on the porch and stared up, his finger poised on the doorbell. Maybe he should have called. Maybe he should just go away. It felt so odd, standing in front of his own house like an intruder. He took a deep breath and rang the bell.

He could hear her footsteps on the stairs, the sound of the locks and latches. He'd put them there for safety, but now it seemed their only purpose was to keep them apart.

The door opened just a crack. "Brian!"

She was smiling. Surprise? Was she glad to see him?

"Hi." He couldn't keep the grin off his face. She looked so good. He wanted to take her into his arms, to kiss her, to feel her softness. But he held back, shoving his hands into his jacket pockets. "Can I come in?"

She laughed—light and breezy—the way he remembered, the way he'd never forgotten. "Sorry." She opened the door wide.

She was wearing his robe, the forest-green terry cloth one, its shoulders swooping down her arms, the sleeves covering her hands, the bottom brushing the floor. It was loosely belted and crisscrossed in a low V at her breasts. Brian felt his heart leap with hope. She was wearing the gold chain—his anniversary gift.

Her hair fell in loose waves to her shoulders. His fingers ached with the memory of its silky softness, then burned with a desire to feel it once again. And her lips—full and softly pink. His own mouth grew moist with wanting.

"When did you get back to Boston?" She'd wanted to say, *home.*

"Yesterday." He met her eyes and saw that they were rimmed with red. "Did I wake you?"

She shook her head and her hair tumbled into her face. "No." She laughed. "I'm reading a physical therapy journal in a desperate attempt to fall asleep."

Brian suggested a recent best-seller he'd used as his bromide. "Works like a charm."

"I'll get it from the library."

"I'll give you my copy."

Her hands were nervously tugging at her hair. "Would you like some coffee?"

"Yes."

They sat down at the kitchen table and it seemed as if he'd never left. How many cups of coffee had they drunk at this table? How many hours had they spent talking, planning, laughing? Brian noticed the dinner dishes piled up in the sink. A big pot of noodles and sauce were still on a burner, and its contents reassured him. Pasta Premarathon—the other half.

"You look great," Ashby said. His hair was longer than normal, coming just over his ears and tumbling over his eyes. He kept pushing it back. And his skin looked taut and weathered. He was trim, and his shoulders hunched forward, the way they did when he was tired. She had the impulse to place her palms on his shoulders, massaging them the way he liked. But she restrained herself.

"So do you." His eyes did a slow tour, each inch familiar, each inch new.

"How's your leg?"

"Good as new."

She smiled with relief. "Then you're running tomorrow?"

He gave an odd shrug.

Ashby clasped the steaming coffee cup between her hands. "I wrote to you." Her eyes burned with the question *Why didn't you answer?*

"I didn't get your letters. I didn't stay at Dan's." He shrugged again.

"Oh."

"Ashby?" He wanted to ask but was afraid. He met her eyes, saw the deep blue turning liquid. He asked, "What did you say... in the letters?"

She hesitated. What if he'd come to ask for a separation? She lifted her chin. "I wrote that I loved you," she said simply. "I realized you were more precious than Olympic gold." Her lips trembled. "Brian, I never stopped loving you."

Tears welled in his eyes. Unmanly, he thought as he happily blinked them away.

"About Roger.... There was never..."

He held up a hand. "I know. I was a fool. It was easier to blame him than face the truth. It wasn't Roger I was jealous of, but your success. After Florida, all that attention, I felt diminished." His eyes grew sad. "I became just your husband."

"I was so insensitive."

He shook his head as he met her eyes. "It took me awhile to realize that being your husband was what I am most proud of."

"You are?"

"Yes, very proud. I lost sight of how much pleasure I got from being your husband and your coach. But tonight I realized what I really wanted. I want to help you become great. I want to see you go for the gold."

Ashby stared at the table. "Right now, it doesn't look very good. I'm in an awful slump. I'm not sure I'll run fast enough to qualify." Her eyelids creased with pain. "You were right, Brian. It's not the coach or the shoes or what I eat that determines whether I make it. It's just me."

He shook his head. "No," he said softly, "not just you." He took her hand and held it very tightly. "It's us. We're gonna do it together. Tomorrow I'm gonna coach you through."

She shook her head. "You have enough to worry about with your own race. It's not fair to you. I've been so selfish, thinking only about my running. This race is something I have to do on my own."

Brian stood up, tall and proud. Suddenly the lines on his face smoothed. He smiled and felt at peace with the decision that had been forming all evening—if not for weeks. "I'm not running tomorrow," he said simply.

"But you said your leg was fine."

"It is."

"Then why?"

"Midcourse correction. The way I figure it, there was nothing wrong with our plan of both of us going for the Olympics—just our timetable. The problem was trying to do it at the same time. So this will be your time. We'll both work to get you to the Olympics. Then in four years I'll have my chance."

She was shocked. She opened her mouth, but nothing came out. "Brian," she finally managed, "this was your dream! I won't let you give it up."

"I'm not. I'm just postponing it for a while."

"Anything can happen by the next Olympics, another injury. . ."

He shrugged. "I'll take that chance. Besides, I'm still getting better, and marathon runners have long careers. Carlos Lopes won the gold medal at thirty-seven. Ashby, your chances will never be better. This is your year. Besides, I want kids. Soon. Right after the Olympics."

"Brian, are you certain that you want to do this?"

"I've never been more sure of anything."

Her face paled. "If I don't make it, I'll have failed us both."

"You won't fail," he said flatly. "I'm sure!"

"You are?"

"Very sure." He took her into his arms, and nothing had ever felt as good, as right as having her small, lithe body against him, running his hand through her hair and smelling its flowery fragrance once again. "Just like

I'm very sure of something else." He flashed a lopsided grin.

"What's that?" she asked, melting against him.

"That I want to make love."

She gave a small frown. "The night before a marathon. Roger wouldn't . . ."

He silenced her with a long kiss, sweeping his hand down her back. "Then I guess we're about to disprove one of Roger's famous theories," he said gleefully.

BRIAN STOOD outside the bathroom door, listening to the toilet flushing one more time. "Ashby, are you okay?"

Her cry rose above the rush of running water. "Wouldn't you know it, the dreaded runs! At the worst possible time!"

"Always strikes when you're most nervous," Brian said through the door.

"It's hopeless. The only record I'm gonna break is most pit stops in a marathon."

"You'll be fine. I've got some of that stuff from when we were in Mexico. Worked on Montezuma's revenge, should knock out a case of nervous stomach. Don't worry, you'll be at the finish line before you know it."

The bathroom door opened. Ashby stood there in her warm-ups, looking pale and nervous. "In this condition, the only line I'll make it to is the waiting line for the portable toilets." She lifted her hands. "Help!"

Brian rummaged through the medicine cabinet until he found a bottle of thick, pink medicine. "Here," he said, measuring it into a spoon. "This'll do it."

"Ugh, that awful stuff."

He waved the bottle threateningly. "It's this, or you'll be baring your buns behind every bush from Hopkinton to the Hancock Tower."

"Okay," she acquiesced, swallowing the pasty liquid and quickly washing it down with water.

"To be on the safe side, you should probably take it again just before the start." He put it on the table along with other emergency supplies.

"Have you been outside?" she asked.

"Yes."

"What's it like?"

"Cool."

"Good!"

"And pouring."

"Damn!" She moaned. "That slows the pace."

REGARDLESS of how many marathons she ran, Ashby knew Boston would always be special. It had a mystique all its own, set apart from all other marathons by tradition and prestige. It had been run continuously since 1897, and the 8021 runners who today swelled the streets of the normally sleepy, white-washed town of Hopkinton, the start of the 26.21875 mile trek to Boston, were among the world's most elite.

As Ashby jogged and jostled her way across the town common, a fine rain fell, making the sky an even gray. But the weather did little to dampen spirits. The air was electric. Each runner was there to fulfill a personal dream, to set a personal best, to show that he or she could still run Boston at fifty or seventy, to triumph over an injury or illness, or merely to earn a badge of honor—to have run Boston and finished.

As Ashby took her place at the starting line, her own dreams were utmost in her mind and her stomach fluttered with nerves. That the race was an important hurdle to becoming an Olympic contender was only part of what it meant to her. More importantly, it symbolized her renewed bond to Brian. He had put his faith in her, entrusted her with their dream. He had sacrificed his dream for her. Today she was running for both of them. And if she failed, she would fail both of them.

She jogged in place, trying to burn off nervous energy. Why had she let Brian talk her into this? She reached beneath her singlet and felt for the chain, the #1, and rubbed her thumb over the charm as if it were a rabbit's foot. She closed her eyes and said a silent prayer. She hoped his faith was not misplaced.

Brian had been conferring with Roger and now he snaked his way toward her. His practiced eyes did a swift assessment. She was wearing a sleek, silver rain jacket and navy shorts. Her hair was pulled into a ponytail. Brian frowned. Her face was pasty white.

"You okay?" he asked, worried.

"I think so," she said as she wiped her damp hands on her jacket.

"Your stomach?"

Ashby glanced toward the Porta-Johns. "Empty, I think."

Brian checked his watch. Eleven-fifty. Ten minutes till the start. He pasted a tape onto her wrist. It contained her splits—her target times for critical distances. "Now remember, check your splits and try to run at the pace we set. Don't worry about who's ahead or behind. You don't have to win or set records—just finish in under two-fifty."

"Got it?"

She nodded, bent down and retied her shoe laces for the tenth time.

He grinned and patted her bottom. "Good luck! I'll be waiting for you just past Ripley Street, the top of the hill—twenty miles."

She nodded grimly.

"One more thing." His face softened into a tender smile. "Whatever happens, remember I love you."

She looked up, warmed by his love. "I know," she said, smiling into his soft, green eyes.

"YOU'RE HALFWAY," Roger's assistant, Kim said, running alongside as Ashby quickly gulped water. "Your time's 84.20 minutes." Ashby glanced at her wrist, where her splits were written. She was badly off her projected pace.

If she ran the second half at the same pace, she would just squeak in under the qualifying time. But she'd run the easy part. The dreaded hills, the fatigue, the wall, were still to come.

"Try to pick it up," Kim urged, doing her best not to appear alarmed. "Give yourself a margin, in case you hit the demons later on."

"But I've already hit the demons," Ashby mumbled as she threw her cup onto the ground and kept running.

She had gotten a sluggish start, running the first five miles as if drugged, her body refusing to warm, to find its natural rhythm. Despite her urging, her coaxing, her pleading, her body had resisted her commands to go fast and had settled into a middling pace. Ashby watched in quiet desperation as other runners streamed past. *Don't think about them*, she told herself. *You only have to beat the clock.*

It didn't help that her head throbbed and that her stomach cramped. Maybe Roger had been right, she thought. Maybe she should have skipped the race. But it was too late for maybes. She was in it, and there was no turning back. And up ahead—just seven miles—Brian was waiting at the top of the hill, and she didn't intend to let him down. *Them down*, she thought, as she gritted her teeth and willed her feet forward, faster.

A MOBILE RADIO had relayed Ashby's times, and Brian wore a worried frown. It was touch and go, and she still had the hard second half. He paced back and forth, then jogged, as if he could somehow run for her. Damn, if he hadn't gone away, if he'd come back sooner, if he'd been there to coach her, she wouldn't have fallen into this dismal slump.

He closed his eyes, fixed a picture of Ashby in his mind and willed her his energy. *Come on, Champ, you can do it, you can do it for us.*

ASHBY GAZED with alarm at the mobile minicam that was aimed at her. The TV camera crew was no surprise. It routinely tracked the elite runners, and the proximity of the camera would not normally have disturbed her. It was just that at the very moment when the camera had fixed its close-up lens on her, she'd been scanning the landscape in a desperate search for an appropriate pit stop. She'd forgotten to take a final dose of Brian's Montezuma miracle, and her stomach lurched and gurgled ominously.

Unless the van moved on very soon, she faced the dubious honor of seeing her least proud moment—a desperate dash—broadcast on the nightly news. Her stomach cramped, her breathing tight, she strained to hear the announcer. She blinked her eyes with relief as she heard his wrap-up and gave a huge sigh as the vehicle moved ahead. When she was safely out of camera range, she bolted.

A SOFT RAIN was falling. The temperature had dropped several degrees. The wind picked up and was whistling through the still bare trees. Despite his sweater and his windbreaker Brian shivered. But the chill was coming from within. He was shivering with fear.

He turned his attention to the throng fighting its way uphill. He pulled his collar up; the wind was coming at his back. *His back.* He froze. The wind had shifted. It was blowing hard against the pack. Ashby would be running uphill into the wind. He tightened his hand into a fist and punched the air. "Why now?" he moaned. "Why now?"

ASHBY'S LEGS stiffened and knotted as she banked into the first section of Heartbreak Hill. She was running at full speed, fighting the wind, trying desperately to make up for lost time. The hills weren't the best place to try to gain time, but at this point—sixteen miles—she didn't have much choice. She thought it ironic that along its most difficult stretch the route passed first a hospital, then a cemetery. She kept her eyes trained in front as she passed those sinister markers. But even so, as the route climbed and climbed, it felt like sudden death.

BRIAN LOOKED at his watch again; he was worried. He should have seen her minutes ago, and each second that ticked away made the outcome seem bleaker. His face brightened as he caught sight of a woman struggling up the hill. He held his breath and shut his eyes, hoping, praying. But when he opened them, his face fell. The woman was now clearly in view. And it was not Ashby.

A CRAMP, a stitch in the side. *Please, not now when every second counts.* She tried for a deep breath and felt daggerlike pains in her side. She pressed her hand hard against the cramp. Common sense told her to slow, to walk. But she faced Hobson's choice: if she ran slowly enough to ease the cramp, she'd run too slowly to qualify. Sweat poured down her forehead, and she ignored the urgent plea of her body to go slowly. She would not slow, she would not walk. She would run to the top. She couldn't bear to have Brian see her walking.

ASHBY! Thank God! Her face was creased in pain, her step uneven, but she was running amazingly fast. Brian unscrewed the cap on the water bottle and jogged toward her. Her eyes sparkled with relief when she spotted him and she managed a cheerful smile. She grabbed the bottle. "How hopeless is it?" she asked.

"You're over the worst," he said as he ran alongside. "Just six miles more."

"My time?"

He gritted his teeth. "Two-twelve."

She calculated quickly. "That leaves six miles in thirty-eight minutes."

He nodded soberly.

"I've never run the last six that fast."

"Not yet," he corrected. "You can do it. Come on. I'll run with you for a while."

"Thanks!"

Brian search desperately for some bit of advice or encouragement that might help. But what, he wondered, could make her run faster than hell? A smug smile curled his lips. That day along the river when they'd raced that final mile, she'd run like a bat out of hell. His smile widened into a naughty grin. "You make it over that line in under two-fifty, I'll do anything, any fantasy at all."

"Oh God, Brian, if I make it, my only fantasy will be to be carried off, to never even walk again."

"Meet you at the finish with a hot fudge sundae," he teased.

"Whipped cream, too?"

"Sure. Anything. I'll be your sex slave."

She grabbed her side. "Don't make me laugh, it hurts."

"I promise you a seduction even Cleopatra would envy. Close your eyes and fantasize."

Fantasize in the middle of the Boston Marathon? He must be crazy! But she closed her eyes. *Floating down a river, carried along by a bevy of strong men, rowing, racing at top speed, faster and faster. And in the front, the coxswain—bronzed, muscled, glistening.* She felt a sudden surge. She was moving fast, still faster. As hard as she could, then harder.

THE DRIZZLE turned to a hard rain. Ashby wiped the water from her eyes, brushed her wet hair off her forehead and wondered what in the world she'd ever liked about running. She'd shed her rain gear miles back, and now her shorts and T-shirt were soaked through. But she was almost there, just a little more than a mile. Just a little more than six minutes. Just a little more than a snowball's chance in hell. But she wasn't about to give up while an ounce of strength remained.

Her name. *Suzanne.* She was hearing voices. She was so exhausted, she was hallucinating. In other marathons she'd hit the wall, had the heaves, but never voices. *Suzanne, Suzanne.*

It wasn't unusual to hear her name. The program, hawked by vendors, listed runners by number and name. But she was listed as Ashby, not Suzanne. Only one person called her that, only one person had that high, proper voice. But she couldn't possibly be here.

With growing panic Ashby rubbed her eyes. But now there was no mistake. Standing in front of the barricade, collar pulled up, her expensive fur coat pathetically drenched, her Italian leather boots ruined by rain, was Elizabeth Clayton. Her hand was stretched high above her head, and as Ashby blinked back tears, she saw that her mother was waving a small banner—the flag of the Olympic games.

Her vision cleared, and Ashby met her mother's eyes—sapphire blue to sapphire blue. And her mother dabbed her eyes with a handkerchief. Her mother, in the shivering cold, watched her daughter, her pain.

Ashby squared her weary shoulders and lifted her chin proudly. She wouldn't let her mother see her pain, feel her anguish. Her hands shot above her head in a triumphant V. Her mother, Brian, they believed in her! And somehow she would make it. She would not let them down. As her mother dissolved into a glorious blur, Ashby shot ahead.

She was flying, her arms and legs pumping, her chest heaving as she desperately gulped air. The last half mile, five hundred yards. And then just ahead the sheer facade of glass—the Hancock Tower, the end.

The crowd, ten deep, cheered her on as she sprinted the final yards, the final feet, their energy, their good wishes carrying her along to the finish. And as Ashby crossed the finish line, her time flashed onto the giant, digital clock: 2:49:35. Twenty-five seconds to spare.

But the memory that Ashby was to cherish came seconds later. As she collapsed into Brian's proud arms, she heard the announcer's voice over the loud speaker.

"Ashby O'Hara, the wife of Boston runner Brian O'Hara, has just qualified for the Olympic trials."

Epilogue

BRIAN O'HARA stood on the sidelines as the photographers snapped pictures of the American women's Olympic marathon team. Just hours ago, competing against two hundred twenty-three elite runners, Ashby had finished second in the women's Olympic marathon trials, winning one of the three coveted places on the team.

Brian beamed with fierce pride. They'd done it—the first part of their Olympic dream. More than a year after her qualifying race in Boston, Ashby O'Hara had become an Olympian. In two more months, she'd be representing the U.S. in Madrid.

Then they'd work on the second phase of their dream: getting Brian a place on the team for the next Olympics.

Brian smiled as his eyes ran down Ashby's brand-new red, white and blue warm-ups, then broadened into a large grin as his eyes rested on her throat. The antique gold chain, his anniversary gift, hung around her neck, and dangling from it was Aunt Amanda's sapphire pendant. Brian had presented it to her on their trip to the Virgin Islands last year. Other people probably thought that the delicate pendant looked a bit odd atop

the utilitarian uniform, but to Brian it looked just perfect.

A hand clapped his shoulder. "Congratulations."

He turned, smiling as he recognized Ted McDowell.
Brian thought that the sportswriter looked perhaps a
little older. But it had been more than a year since he'd
seen him. "Thanks," he said. "I'm thrilled with the as-
signment." Brian had been hired by a television network to do color commentary of the Olympic track and
field events. It meant he'd be in Madrid with Ashby—
covering her race, sharing her glory days.

McDowell chuckled softly. "I didn't mean the as-
signment," he explained, resting his eyes on Ashby. He
offered his outstretched hand. "What I meant is, you've
won, after all." His voice was a husky whisper. "And
what you've got means more than the gold."

Brian ignored McDowell's hand. Instead he wrapped
the older, wiser man in a tight embrace. "I know," Brian
said, his heart so full with joy, he thought it might
break. "I know."

COMING NEXT MONTH

#309 AFTER HOURS Gina Wilkins

Executive assistant Angelique St. Clair knew the office
gossips said she and her boss, Rhys Wakefield, were made
for each other; they were both cold, intimidating
workaholics. And maybe they were—during business
hours. But after hours, the heat they generated was enough
to melt a polar ice cap . . . and the heart of one very
cool CEO!

#310 TALISMAN Laurien Berenson

Woodbury, Connecticut, wasn't New York City. And Kelly
Ransome wasn't a city woman. She was straightforward
and freshly scrubbed . . . and came equipped with three
Dobermans! But that didn't stop journalist Eric Devane
from pursuing her. After all, Eric had an overexuberant
Rotweiller pup on his hands, and Kelly was a dog trainer—
the best. And Eric Devane *only* pursued the best.

#311 HIDDEN MESSAGES Regan Forest

Vacationing on a Scottish isle, Laurie MacDonald fell in
love with Eric Sinclair—part Gypsy, part rogue and all sex
appeal. But then she discovered his love was a deception
and she plotted a fitting revenge . . . only she couldn't
convince her heart she was better off without him.

#312 ALWAYS Jo Morrison

Tanner McNeil wanted a wife. After eight years of trying to
convince footloose Jodi to settle down with him on the
farm, he'd given up. Meeting Lara Jamison restored his
hope in happy endings. But Lara suspected that perfect as
they were for each other in bed, Tanner was still seeing Jodi
in his dreams. . . .

HARLEQUIN
American Romance®

THE LOVES OF A CENTURY

Join American Romance in a nostalgic look back at the twentieth century—at the lives and loves of American men and women from the turn-of-the-century to the dawn of the year 2000.

Journey through the decades from the dance halls of the 1900s to the discos of the seventies . . . from Glenn Miller to the Beatles . . . from Valentino to Newman . . . from corset to miniskirt . . . from beau to significant other.

Relive the moments . . . recapture the memories.

Watch for all the CENTURY OF AMERICAN ROMANCE titles in Harlequin American Romance. In one of the four American Romance books appearing each month, for the next ten months, we'll take you back to a decade of the twentieth century, where you'll relive the years and rekindle the romance of days gone by.

Don't miss a day of A CENTURY OF AMERICAN ROMANCE.

A CENTURY OF
AMERICAN ROMANCE
1910s

The women . . . the men . . . the passions . . . the memories . . .

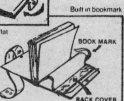

COMING SOON

In September, two worlds will collide in four very special romance titles. Somewhere between first meeting and happy ending, Dreamscape Romance will sweep you to the very edge of reality where everyday reason cannot conquer unlimited imagination—or the power of love. The timeless mysteries of reincarnation, telepathy, psychic visions and earthbound spirits intensify the modern lives and passion of ordinary men and women with an extraordinary alluring force.

Available in September!

EARTHBOUND—Rebecca Flanders
THIS TIME FOREVER—Margaret Chittenden
MOONSPELL—Regan Forest
PRINCE OF DREAMS—Carly Bishop

DRSC-RR